UNSEEN

"A journey to find yourself"

PRATYUSA ROY

ISBN 979-8-89233-391-7

This book is dedicated to three very different people. Firstly my husband Sagnik, Thank you for putting up with those extreme anxious nights where I loiter around the house looking for that one perfect word. Secondly Debkanya, my friend my colleague without whom I would have lost midway. And lastly my old friend with whom I discussed doing this in college, Akash. Thank you for inspiring me and lending me two of your most brilliant poetry and all those brainstorming sessions. Without you three this book wouldn't be one!

CONTENTS

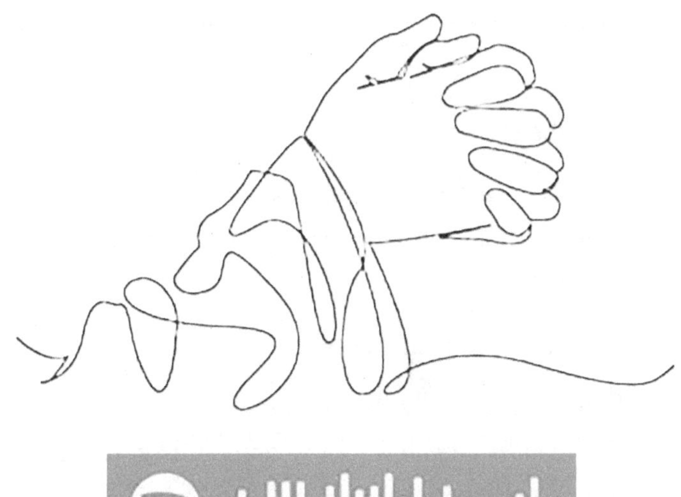

Chapter 1

SO MUCH FOR A GOOD NIGHT'S SLEEP!

Neon lights. Blue. Pink. Burning cigarettes. Moist lips. 'Apocalypse'. by 'Cigarettes after sex'. She was in a red laced lingerie. Lonely. Feeling the numbness of the situation. Her eyes looked tired. Her mind, restless though. She poured some whiskey. Three cubes of ice.

She rubbed her lips around the edge of the glass as if she wanted it to bite back. Disappointed that it didn't, she gulped the alcohol. She should sleep now, otherwise she would be late for her job the next morning, but she wanted to snatch some more time from her boring life. Some more moments.

"Hi" she texted a friend.

They have a history and tension. I love stories that have tension. She bit her lips, thinking about all the possibilities.

"Hey! Ssup?" came the reply

"Not much, really bored. You?" she typed while thinking about what she would've done if they were talking in person.

I am sure he was thinking about it too.

"Yeah, same…" he replied,

And a lot of tension…

She hesitated to move forward from this point. Because once done, they cannot stop it. It's like a moth attracted towards the fire, craving for the warmth, and the pain, and finding pleasure in that.

If you ask me, there's no point in hesitating now, she should have hesitated before texting "hi" now she's already trapped in a Mindspace where she wants it all.

But the more interesting part is what's stopping her. In her mind she craves for this, day in day out.

"I am Kinda drunk" she texted pouring another drink.

She is not a teenager who can blame anything and everything on alcohol. She knows that. Yet her impulse was too strong to resist. Her hair draping over her neckline, making this night more irresistible. 'If he were here', she thought and deliberately put her hair back exposing her collarbone. the cool touch of the whiskey glass against her skin released the knotted heat within,

"Yeah, how much?" he asked... I wonder why?

All physical objects that are in contact can exert force on each other. If one of the objects exerting the force happens to be a rope, string, chain, or cable we call the force **tension**. But here it was "NO STRINGS ATTACHED" or was it? Can best friends be 'no strings attached'?

The law of physics tends to break before a chemical reaction...

He is forbidden, which makes him sexier.

She has always been a rebel, sometimes without a cause. It's intimidating. The idea of being different.

"Well so much to do this"

She sent the text along with a picture, a picture of her in the red lingerie, the pink shade was falling on the highlights of her body, and the blues were like diving deep into the cleavages of her skin. The delicate lace added an extra layer of allure. She knows exactly how to play around now.

“damn” he said.

Honestly, she is so tired of her cover of being a ‘good girl’. She is ready to be fearless, shameless...

Thinking about him can make her so wet, imagine what would physical touches do?

She now knows exactly what he likes and how. She wants to give her all up for this. for that touch. He knows exactly how to tease her. How to keep her hanging. And honestly what’s the fun if you get everything at one time?

She is well aware of his longings and style; he would kiss her lips like a dessert. She would burn from inside. Maybe he would pull apart, just to make her beg for it. Maybe her hand would be exploring him, from his shiny but messy hair to the back of his ears. And when his hands will be unhooking the lingerie from behind his Toung will rest on her neck. Warm breaths will send her chills down her spine. Maybe she would unbutton him, hand him over the belt he was wearing. He would use the belt like a collar when she would go down on him. She knows he will enjoy, when she would occasionally look up with her mouth full of him. He would make her stand by the wall with her ass standing out, maybe spank her. He would press her against the wall, putting her hands above her head. He would place his dick at the opening of her cunt and thrust it inside. And with each stroke she would moan his name Lauder. The rythm would be madning. Until both shatter like filled glass, from inside.

Everyone writes about the calmness before the storm? Have you ever heard the calmness after a storm? Satisfying. Mind numbing.

So much for a good night sleep huh?

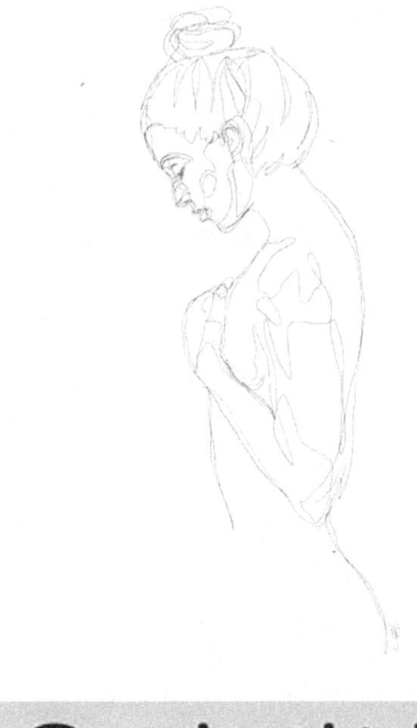

Chapter 2

THE BITCH WHO ESCAPED HELL!

9.30. alarm snoozed. 9.45. snoozed. 9.50. she struggles to open her eyes. But she knows she has to. She pulled herself up from the bed anyhow. Rubbed her eyes. Kohl from under eyes got smudged, more. She forgot to take off her makeup last night. She covered herself with a robe hanging in the side bar. She lives alone, the idea of walking around naked is arousing. but she cannot feel that right now. She has a crazy day at work. Some important deals to crack. She pulled herself together. From a bitch who escaped hell to a working woman. She couldn't be late today. She poured herself a cup of coffee because she knew that's the only thing that keeps her running this morning.

She worked hard that day, harder than other days. Maybe, she was trying to escape her own mind about last night. She didn't allow the gap from which guilt can come in. A crack from which morals can play their card game and win. She made peace with the restlessness. But she cannot do it with guilt. Especially when it's not the first time.

Phone rang. "babe". She looked at the call.

"Good morning" she said

"Good morning, I love you" he said. Not the friend from last night. Boyfriend.

"I love you too" she said with a faint smile and fake enthusiasm.

"Hectic day at work? Do you want me to order some food for you babe?"

"No, I am fine, will talk later, someone is calling me, bye, love you" she disconnected the call.

Chapter 3

THE GUY WITH A SMILE

'Falling in love at a coffee shop' by 'Landon Pigg'. Have you ever felt so positive talking to someone? Someone that you never met, someone you don't know. A complete stranger. And you actually start trusting the stranger over the people you had in your life before. Someone who exactly meets all your criteria from the fantasy you always had. Feels like a dream, no?

She was going through a similar phase. Remember when I told you how complicated her story was, wait I actually never did, but anyway, she had a lot inside her, sexually mainly, emotionally too. She wanted to be seen, she wanted to be heard, and she wanted to be praised. For a very long time, she was craving all of this, her boyfriend loves her so much, puts all her needs in front of everything, he is always there for her she knows. But still, she felt unseen, unheard.

A lonely Monday afternoon. Monotony brings out the devil in her. Her fingers stopped on a website where people can strip, she never had the fear of the unknown, instead she always found comfort in them.

'Tempting,'

she thought. She immediately, out of curiosity, opened the website. Maya. She registered as maya. Obviously, it's not her real name. She is very confused. Like you remember the first time you drove a car, that was kind of confusing. The website is cheap.

She was wearing a comfortable camisole. Feeling adrenaline running through her blood. Suddenly she got a private chat request from some mcdreamyxxX. Dwelling upon the thought for a little, biting her lip, a little harder, she accepted.

A guy, with the webcam on, had a smile. Not what she expected. She hesitated. On second thought, she turned on her camera too. The guy smiled again. Her heart skipped a beat. She expected objectification. A little womanizing comment, she expected graphic content. Weird right? strip website, chaos, noise from the road nearby, and all you notice is the smile. It happens sometimes. Rarely.

"Hello maya"

"Hello" she said, still confused.

"You look beautiful" he typed smiling to the camera!

Her heart skipped again.

"I like Indian girls" He wrote again

This freaked her out, is he a crazy stalker who already knows her location? thousands of thoughts crossed her mind..

"How do you know?" she typed with trembling hands.

"Your profile says so..." he smiled again and winked to the camera.

'*cute*', she thought.

"Where are you from?" she asked

"Guess..."

"USA?"

"Not really, a country of pyramids"

She is so intrigued by Mr. mcdreamyxxX that she couldn't think rationally. It took her a while to process...

"You went to my profile" he said,

She smiled hesitantly.

"Egypt it seems"

"Right kiddo" he smirked

Kiddo. Such a small word. Do you feel a word has the strength of making you feel so secure?

Yes, that's what she felt.

The sense of security she felt with a stranger she did not feel with anybody else.

Chapter 4

RUM AND RESIN

'Iris' by 'Goo goo dolls' A lovely monsoon day. Earphones and window seat. Excited. Scared. Brave.

Why? Why so many emotions at the same time?

I know you are thinking, what did she do now? Let me break it down for you.

Earlier today...

"Hey, you look different" a senior from her college replied on her WhatsApp story.

"Like good different or bad different?" she replied.

The sudden validation was like when you bite liquor chocolate. The bitter-sweet taste of it.

"Like hot different" came the reply.

Her cheeks flushed. She felt seen. If only I could tell her that she does not need any gratification to feel hot I would, I know for a fact that she won't listen to me.

"Do you want to meet by any chance?" he asked.

His name is Rudh, he used to play for a renowned Bengali football club under 19. She has a sweet relation with this guy. He was friendly. They always acted like frenemies. To be very honest, Rudh was the one of very few people she was close to during her initial college days. Though he was his senior, they felt like friends.

Him asking her out was surprising and validating for her. Also, scary. He belongs to an enemy territory. A classic senior junior conflict!

"Like today?" she knew what she wanted...

Wait, is it a date? No, it's not. Committed people won't go on dates with others. It is a casual meeting between two casual friends, but what would she tell her not-so-casual boyfriend? She doesn't want to think about her boyfriend right now.

'If everything's made to be broken, she just wants to know who she was"

"Yeah, choose a place, we'll meet at 6" I am sure he felt the same emotions she felt inside her stomach. Or did he?

She was a classis blend of allure and brain. But she always underestimated her beauty. Maybe that came from her past skinny shaming experience and bullies in high school. She always thought her brain and heart were her best features. She never played dumb in front of a guy. But is Rudh, genuinely interested in her? Or is this gonna be a physical affair? Or a friendly date?

Six in the evening is a little late for a person who has a curfew time set by her boyfriend.

But she was determined because her heart wanted a friendly face. She wanted comfort. And well, if she is doing this to her boyfriend, why do it only with that friend?

Next thing you know, she was wearing a blue off-shoulder top, skinny jeans, high heels, on that bus, near the second last window seat, she looked stunning.

"Hey, long time no see..." she said while hugging Rudh when she met him.

"What can I do? Been busy replying to people's WhatsApp stories" he said charmingly

Loud music, neon lights, shots, occasional eye contact.

"You remember the fashion show?" he asked

"How can I forget! Both my real life and stage partner sucked" she complained

"Hey common, you ditched us really bad"

"I know, I felt really bad about it,"

She remembers everything as if it was yesterday, Rudh introduced her to the fashion club. And she was the perfect fit. They had a gig before their fresher's party. They put their blood and sweat, practicing countless hours for the show.

It was important for her. Her heart craved exposure and freedom. The fashion show was the closest to her tick boxes she created while growing up watching cringe shows.

But for a 23-year-old man, his 18 years old girlfriend hanging around with a bunch of guys, having fun laughing, being glamorous sounds frightening. Or does it? she remembered hoe after every practice session she used to fight with her boyfriend. How his dad suddenly became sick on the day of her show. How she was emotionally manipulated not to go. How he had a problem when she felt seen.

"it's okay, its water under the bridge now" he reassured,

She should not think about the past now, she is here to have fun. She looks around, people are having a good time.

She pours the 6th shot down her throat. And looked at him. He is actually a charming man.

"Let's go for a smoke" he proposed after three to four more rounds of shots.

Suddenly the world around her looked so free. She forgot when was the last time she laughed like this. She felt comfortable in her soul. She felt beautiful in his gaze.

Men are understanding and not in their own way. The beauty of this makes them more humane.

He took her hands and took her to the smoking room of the pub. He lit up the cigarettes and the yellow flame cast a gentle glow on his face. His eyes, his smile, the way he lifts up his eyebrows. With each puff of the cigarette, the tension in the air grew stronger. He smells amazing. A mixture of a woody smell with tinge of vanilla.

"Hey, do you have a lighter," a Stanger asked making her conscious of the distance between them.

Here you go," he replied, handing him the lighter and offering help in lighting his cigarette.

"Thanks man, first date?" the stranger asked

He smiled a little and looked at her.

"Is it that obvious?" he said. eyes still on her.

"I am here with my girlfriend and her best friend. Have fun man"

They shook hands. She was a little tipsy. He clasped her waist like a gentle-man.

Everything was out of focus. She could feel the warmth of his breath on her shoulders when they sat down.

"First date huh?" she gave him a side eye

"Is it not?" he gazed into her eyes. A hint of a smile tugging at the corner of his lips.

She looked at his eyes, for a second it felt like her eyes were looking for a different ones.

He brushes his thumb on her lips and her skin dotted with goosebumps. Slowly, he leaned in, closing the distance between them until his lips met hers in that first. He tasted like rum and Rasin. He hastily pulled apart to ask for consent maybe. She bit her lips in desire. She kissed him this time. Their lips met like two puzzle pieces. For the first time in a very long time, she felt like not stopping. All caged up emotions and desires ran wild inside her.

Before anyone threw them out of the pub, they quickly settled the bill and made their way to his car.

They were inseparable. Their bodies gravitate towards one another, their hands exploring each other's contours as they kiss passionately. lips. Toung. Neck. The windows begin to fog up shielding them from prying eyes. Her nimble fingers worked their way down his shirt, one button at a time, revealing the sculpted contours of his chest beneath. With each button undone, she leaned in to explore the newly exposed skin with her lips, planting soft kisses along his collarbone and chest. His breathing grew heavier, matching the rhythm of their racing hearts. His hands, still tracing the inside of her thighs, moved upwards, gently sliding beneath her off-shoulder top. The touch of his fingertips on her bare skin was electric.

All good things come to an end.

"I think your pants are vibrating" she said in a funny way when his phone vibrated

exploring the warmth of her skin he said, "That's nothing"

The phone was buzzing continuously. Three times, four times...

"I think you should take it, can be urgent" she suggested

He made a face "It's my mom" He picked up the call.

She got back her senses. She also had twenty missed calls from her boyfriend. However, her focus shifted to a more pressing concern: her phone battery was critically low, with only 2% remaining.

He hangs up the call and looks at her with a 'can't do' look.

"I'll try to book a cab" she said reading the situation "you should go home"

"You sure? You can manage?" he asked

No, she can't manage. She is drunk beyond the limit. Her body doesn't wanna go. Anywhere. It longs for fulfilment. But she was one of those who can shit bricks inside and have a face that says

"Yeah yeah. Don't worry."

He should have dropped her. If not, he should have waited for her, until the uber arrived. But she should have told him to wait. She should have told him her phone was dead. She should have understood she was drunk.

In desire, in love, in life you should ask for the things your heart longs for. You should share the things that scares you. The person opposite you is equally new to this maybe. Her mistake was not to communicate. His mistake? Who are we to judge?

She got out of the car and watched as his car disappeared into the distance. She is on her own now. Drunk. Vulnerable. In her drunken mind, her biggest regret is the decision of wearing the high heels.

She quickly climbs into the taxi and with her mind preoccupied, she may have overlooked the usual practice of sitting in the back seat as a passenger.

Empty roads. drizzle of rain. On her face. Car stereo. 'Hold me now' by 'Red.'

'Hold me now... till the fear is leaving, I am barely breathing...'

She dozed off. She dozed off, in the middle of the night with no phone, no person knowing where she was.

Anything could happen to her. She could have never seen the light of a day. She tossed her entire future ahead of her.

But she learnt something valuable that day. A lesson which will make her a better person. Was this worth the risk? she asked herself...

It was worth it. It is always worth finding out who you are, what you like or how you wanna be touched. It's always right to be selfish sometimes to understand your desires and fantasies.

She discovered a new self that day. From a girl who thought she hated public display of affection to a girl kissing the college stud in public... Who is she?

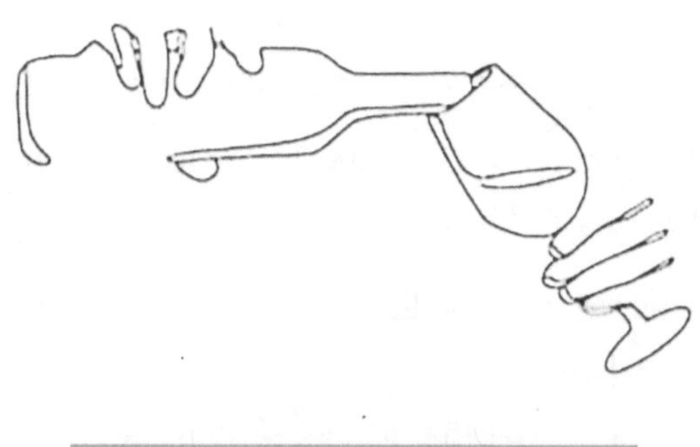

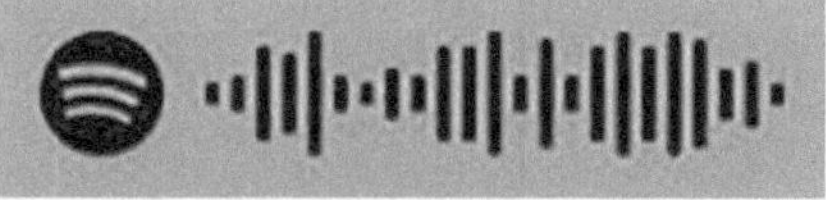

Chapter 5

A REALITY CHECK!

Frizzy hair. Smudged lipstick. Tired eyes. Hangover? Maybe something more. Last night was no one's fault. She understood very well last night, she is out of love with her boyfriend. But she did not have the courage somehow to say it out loud.

Her phone was switched off. She hesitated before putting it in charge. She cannot undergo interrogation right now. Even her strict parents did not call her so many times in a week like her boyfriend did yesterday. She is too hungover to face this right now. And the best way to deal with a hangover is to get hammered. At least that what her senses said

"Can you come home" she texted one of her childhood friend, she wants someone to say things out loud to her.

"What did you do this time?" she asked "Coming in 5 mins. Order food. Do you need vodka"

"Come!" she sends the text with a picture of the vodka bottle in her hand.

She hit herself with two shots of the same before she came. It's called prepping.

"Tell me everything, tell me now. Also, did you order food?" she stormed in

"Pizza, pepperoni, and it's complicated," she said

"It better be Paloma, otherwise I wouldn't have left office and come to your house, to day-drink" She looked at her with judgmental eyes.

Paloma. That's her name.

"Have a drink first?" Paloma said passing her a chilled glass of vodka with lime cordial.

"Don't freak out Shree, I kinda went out with someone" She continued

"What do you mean by you went out? Like a date? Is it Neel? It is Neel. I kinda always knew something is going on between you two"

Neel is her best friend. The friend we spoke about. The one with tension.

"It was not Neel. Yesterday. It was someone else" she made a face. Shree very well knows this face. This is Paloma's 'I messed up' face

"Wait wait! It was not Neel yesterday! That means there is a day with Neel as well" she said while opening the pizza box and pouring oregano on top. She continued "I always knew. But that's not important. Tell me who did you go out with?"

"So, I had a senior in college..."

"Show me! "Shree interrupted paloma.

She started scrolling through her phone until she found good enough photo of Rudh for Shree.

While Shree was busy judging the guy by his looks, if he qualified enough to give up what she gave up, Paloma explained to her the entire story.

"And I am guessing Satya is nowhere in this story" Shree stated looking at her with judgmental eyes.

Satya is the boyfriend FYI.

Paloma and Shree are childhood friends. Shree has seen Paloma like this before. She is still processing. Her feelings. Her judgements. Paloma knew Shree very well. For her, cheating is equal to the corruption of religion. She knows Shree has her own rule book on do's and don'ts's of her life.

Cheating is a big 'no-no' there. There are other rules which make her the person she is.

People can misunderstand Shree, people can think that she's a moral polices, yes, she is passive-aggressive most of the time, but it's the good kind of passive-aggressive which protects you from preying eyes in the pub or texting your ex for the zillionth of the time.

She can be the drama queen and a bitch, but to the people you want her to be a bitch to. but at the end of the day, you would want someone like her in your team to fight your battles on the days you can't.

"Break up with Satya" was the first word that came out of Shree's mouth after the whole story.

Maybe she needed to hear it out loud.

"You are clearly not happy with Satya, that is why you are looking for short term happiness" she continued.

"On top of everything, this is wrong towards Satya. Do you want to be the kind of person who does this to someone?" Shree questioned.

She questioned a lot of things all of a sudden. Shree questioned what kind of a person she was, or at least becoming.

"I... I don't think I can. I need someone. And he... He does not have to know about this. I mean I can always say I passed out or something" she defended. Herself? Or the sudden thoughts Shree has put in her head. Is she really ok with deceiving a man like that?

Shree gulped the alcohol in her glass to digest what paloma just said

"Who are you, Paloma? What have you become? How did this all start?"

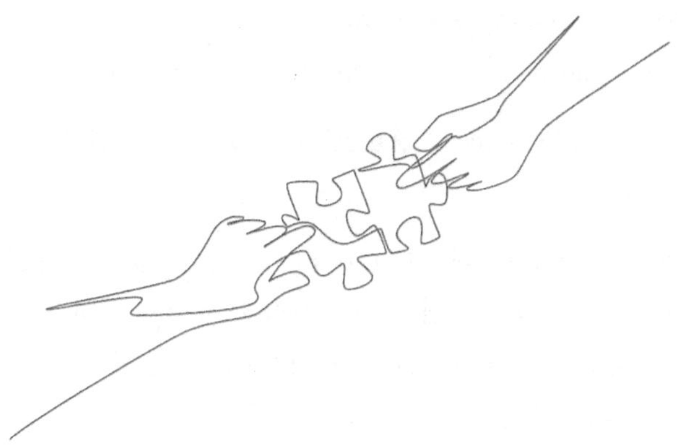

Chapter 6

HOW DID IT ALL START? THE GUY IN A BLUE SHIRT...

'I knew you were trouble' by Taylor Swift. Headphones. coffee in hand. The first day of the second year!

"Can I come in?" she asked in an ignorant tone

She walked in not waiting for a response, while turning off the music.

She looked up to find a seat away from the professor while her eyes landed on someone and everything and everyone around her just vanished. a young gorgeous man, brown eyes, calm. paying attention to the lecture, his blue checkered shirt, different from the college uniform.

Do you believe in love at first sight? She didn't. Until that day.

He couldn't help but notice her. I mean which guy wouldn't notice a girl bamboozled by his own charms? Maybe a smirky smile lingered at the corner of his lips. I am sure he is used to the attention.

She sat down, diagonally behind him. For her, the lecture was more like a muted tv commercial. Not a single word of the professor made sense. She grew restless for it to end.

She knew she wanted to talk to the new guy. At least a formal 'Hi'. But she did not know why.

"*A force that changes the direction of an object towards you, would be a pull. On the other hand, if it moves away, it is a push. Sometimes, force is simply defined as a push or pull upon an object resulting from the object's interaction with another object.*' in this case it was definitely a pull force.

Her heart pounded with a mix of excitement and nervousness. She rehearsed in her head what she would say

"*Hi, my name is Paloma, I haven't seen you around. Are you new here?*" No no, too straightforward.

"*you know we have an uniform!*" too sarcastic...

No no no. she thought She cannot do it, it would be awkward. But she never knew how to act on her impulses. A quick 'hi' wont hurt anyone she thought.

It was only two steps separating them, when he noticed her, for the second time, he stood up from his seat estimating a possible social encounter, their eyes met, and a faint smile graced his lips, she almost opened her mouth to speak. She almost said hi,

Almost!

Her phone began to ring. Disrupting the tension.

A pesky interruption.

The name showed "babe" like the warning sign of a cigarette box. On your face.

She couldn't help but steal a few more seconds to look into those gorgeous brown eyes, before answering the call.

"Hello, yeah, the lecture is over. Oh, you are coming to pick me up. Great. See you." she pretended to be happy, she did not have reasons not to be, "I love you too. Bye!"

She disconnected the call with restlessness inside her. She stared out of the classroom window, and a few seniors were playing football on the ground. Slowly the image faded.

Paloma went into this relationship when she was seventeen years old. Naive, heartbroken. Full of body image issues. The anxiety to 'fit in' gulped her like my young brother eats the last portion of my share. More than it could fit in his mouth.

Satya came to her life like a lifeboat. This is the first time someone showed kindness towards her, the first time someone looked at her affectionately. And just at the right time, when the blackhole was just about to swallow her whole. It had enough water and food to survive. The lifeboat came with rules, if she followed them, she was safe.

They went to the movies together, and they went on bike trips together, drank together, his friends became hers. She learnt new things. It was all roses and pink until the discomfort of being someone else crept in.

"I... I forgot my headphones" a firm voice interrupted her chain of thoughts.

She looked away from the window to find out who the intruder was.

"I am sorry if I..." He chose not to finish the sentence instead he said "Hi, my name is Neel." and extended his right hand towards her.

"Paloma," she said maintaining eye contact. She can look into those eyes for hours. It had the calmness of the ocean waves. She extended her hand as well and they shook hands.

"So, are you new here?" talking suddenly became easy. "Haven't seen you around"

"Today's my first day. In fact, can you guide me to the mechanics' lab?" he asked.

"Just the opposite side of this corridor," she said.

"Come I'll show you" she continued.

They went to the mechanics lab together, while she texted Satya

"Sorry can't come. HOD saw... have to attend this class"

Why did she lie? Why did she not go?

Prorities change with time. And we have to give time a little more time to find out all the whys and hows...

Chapter 7

THE MONSTERS UNDER THE TABLE?

'*Bad liar' by* Imagine dragons. Disco lights. Smell of marijuana mixed with alcohol.

"This is me, all of me," Paloma said, pressing Neel's palms on her chest.

Neel gave her a pride mixed awed smile and pulled away his hands. She is way too drunk to think rationally and he knows that. He always knew she had something for him. But he knew about Satya. From the beginning.

Oh, how did this happen?

After their first encounter, it became easier for Paloma to speak to him. Neel, the love at first sight, started to fill up the massive "friend" sized hole in Paloma's life.

From hanging out in the football ground to drafting their imaginary story (which she totally made up to spend more time with him) in the lonely alleys of the library, unknowingly they were ticking the checkbox of a friendship lifetime. She started smiling genuinly one again.

She shared her scars, and he comforted the wound. The man also came with his unsolved traumas, anxiety and issues and she adopted them. Brownie Point was a gang that came along with it.

Samarth, the carefree (careless) artistic son of a bitch who came as an "Arjun" to our "Karan." The chances of our prime minister answering your phone call are higher than Samarth answering. He will literally text you "What's up?" when your phone is still ringing.

Rouhan, the small-town boy who finally broke free from his father's concentration camp, stays in an apartment with two more men. Football freak thinks Ronaldo is God. But he was the childish one.

Somali, studious, smart, sometimes shellfish full-time sassy young woman. She and Paloma were friends last year as well, but now they have become sisters, which may have made her real sister envy a little.

These are the people who can say black is black and white is white but accept her as grey. Unlike Satya's friends, these were the people with whom Paloma could be her true self. They spoke over con-calls. They texted each other about everything. They celebrated even the smallest victories of each other.

And that day, it was Ruhan's birthday. So, it had to be special. Cheesecake, "blender's sprite" instead of their usual go-to "old monk." Plastic glasses and music. This was the definition of a birthday.

Did Ruhan just become one of the guys his father warned him about while seeing him off?

"House rules!" Neel declared, holding up their glasses. "First peg, 60ml neat shots!"

With grins on their faces, they downed their shots in one go, feeling the drink tickle their throats. The party was lit. With the bottle thoroughly drained, everyone was way past "a little drunk" and deep into the realm of "wildly tipsy." It is beautiful how five different people with their five different meanings of life have five drinks together and blend perfectly.

"Guys, a small toast!" ruhan said with his glass in the air.

And a "whoo" followed.

"Thank you all, for making my day special. You guys are the best thing that happened to me, and thanks to Paloma. Thank God she found Neel cute and became friends with him. Thank God you guys needed a room to sit and chill and I happened to have one. I don't remember how we became so close"

"Cheers to Ruhan's apartment" paloma said with an wink

They all raised their glasses high and clinked them together, the sound of their laughter filling the room.

Meanwhile, Paloma, being Paloma, crawled underneath the study table, maybe to hide from everyone. but guess who followed suit to ensure she was not doing anything stupid? Our brown-eyed prince-charming.

All Paloma could feel was Neel smelled like white chocolate mixed with bourbon. This is the first time she noticed his mole. He has a mole placed in between his lower lips.

Paloma parted her lips" Well, look who's joined me in my little fort! "

"Couldn't let you have all the fun down here, could I? But seriously don't get hurt. You are quite drunk." Neel said with a smirk on his face

"Oh, so you're my guardian angel now, huh?" Paloma teased as she playfully poked her fingers against his cheeks. The smell is driving her crazy. "And I am not that drunk" she claimed

"That's the classic drunk line," Neel protested as he brushed the cigarette ash away from her hair.

The "non-touch" touch torched her like a dry oak wood.

Paloma bit her lip and whispered

"I'm just living in the moment, Neel. After all, it's Ruhan's birthday. And I've got my favorite person right here with me."

She had a habit of unconsciously biting her lips, unaware of the captivating effect it had on those around her.

Neel blushed slightly and replied, "Your favorite person, huh?"

"Speaking of favorites, what's your favorite movie?" he asked, attempting to change the subject. He couldn't flirt with her in good conscience. She might be new to the drinking game, but he was not.

"My favourite movie... Fifty shades darker" she looked away. "And before you say that's porn, it's not. It's a love story, it's a story of how love overcomes traumas," she said passionately, defending her choices.

"I never said it's porn," he said and looked into her eyes for the first time. She was different. Her thoughts were different. For a second did his heart skip a beat? No one knew.

"This is me, all of me" This is her favorite scene from the movie '*Fifty shades darker*' when the male protagonist lets his guard down in front of his love.

Did she put her guard down?

Chapter 8

THE THRESHOLD

Midnight. Messi bun. Strands of hair tickling here and there. She looked beautiful under the candlelight. The flickering flames moved with the breeze. Highlights different parts. Cheekbones sometimes, lips, as she looked towards the empty wall of her room, the streetlights cast a weird shadow. Shadow of the rounded French window opposite the wall. Tears rolled down her cheek, like molten gold. She looked away.

She tried going through the whole conversation with Satya once again. Trying to figure out what went wrong! What can possibly go wrong when you are talking about two fictional characters in a novel?

What do couples talk about? After 3 years of relationship. They know all of each other's secrets, past, heartbreaks and family. After a point, they are left with what happens in their day. Paloma has been reading novels. Mostly because she and Neel are trying to write a story. That was the only way they could spend time together. Only the two of them.

She has finished reading *Charulata* by *Rabindranath Thakur.* For those who are not familiar with the novel, it's a story where 'Charulata' paints a vivid 19th-century Bengali portrait. Charulata is a woman whose emotions and entanglements with her husband's cousin mirror the intricate dance of modern desires, creating a masterpiece of forbidden love and self-discovery.

She just finished the novel when Satya called. Duty call. That's what the gang named these phone calls.

"I just finished reading *Charulata*. Oh my god, what a story! What a character." Paloma did not wait for a 'hello'

"*Charulata*! I watched the movie by Rituparno. Which character are you talking about? I did not find any character that good. But yeah, I like her husband" Satya said reluctantly.

"What do you mean? Charulata herself is the most evolving character in the book." Paloma said passionately

"I hated Charulata. She was the most deceiving woman a man can have in his life. How can you like her? Makes me question your views on relationship" Satya questioned. Her judgment? Her character? What did he question about? His statement/question pierced through her heart. It felt like a personal attack

"Satya, I understand why you might feel that way, but let's talk about Charulata's journey. She wasn't just a 'deceiving woman.' She was trapped in a marriage where her desires and potential were stifled. Her connection with Amal brought out her artistic side, her passion for life." Paloma said in a defensive tone.

"Oh, so you are saying you would do the same thing if I were busy in my work"

"It was not one day her husband got busy. He overlooked her needs. Physical intimacy is a big thing in a relationship Satya!"

"So, you are saying you would do the same thing to me if I were managing work and, life and my family and cannot have sex with you. You are saying you would sleep around?"

It's very difficult to have a different opinion from Satya. It starts like a debate and ends in an argument. It's either his way or a highway. Paloma tries hard to hide her opinions if they differ.

She tried to deviate from the topic. But he kept making personal comments. After a point, she kept listening. Without protesting. It was a relief when Satya said "I have work tomorrow. I can't do this overnight." and he disconnected.

She felt caged. The knot inside her chest is getting bigger day by day. She had so many feelings inside her. Angry, sad, attacked, self-doubt. All she wanted was someone to tell her, it was okay to think differently.

If it was a month back, she would have cried herself to sleep. Go to college with puffy eyes the next morning. Satya would have sent her a nice breakfast and she would have thought it was all okay. But now she has someone, someone who was empathetic towards her.

"Can I call you" she texted.

She couldn't wait for the reply. Impatiently she dialed Neel's number.

Wish you were here. That was his caller tune. Her cheeks hurt from the aggressive wiping of tears.

'A *smile from a veil?*

Do you think you can tell...'

The music discontinued.

"Hello?" a familiar voice numbed her pain. For a second.

"I am sorry if I... good time to talk?" Was he busy? With someone else. Or something else. Is she bothering her? Thoughts like this made her voice crack a little.

"Paloma?" He tried to pull her back from her overthinking session. It worked. He continued "Had a fight with Satya? What happened this time?"

"Can you just be with me for some time? We don't need to talk. About anything." she whimpered.

"Cry it out. I am here." His voice felt like a soft touch. It felt like someone was caressing her.

It's so easy to make someone feel secure and not just by words. A simple gesture can make a lot of difference. She was too young to understand that intimacy is not only the lips, neck and what is under that.

"You want to drink some water?" was intimacy. "Or a cigarette maybe?"

"I don't have a cigarette!" she said with a stuffy nose

"If you stop crying and self-loathing. I can arrange a cigarette for you"

"How" she said, wiping away her tears.

"You remember the other day; we were playing football? And I kept all my stuff inside your bag because I wasn't carrying one."

"Yeah..."

"I left a cigarette in your bag. Thought you might need it someday"

See what I meant by intimacy.

"You did?" a small smile broke out from the corner of her dried and chappy lips.

"Drink some water first" he instructed.

All her sadness vanished just like how the wave of ocean erases the scribbles on the sand. Did he care that much? Or is he like this with everyone?

She lit the cigarette with the almost burnt-out candle.

"You feel better now?" he asked.

"Hmm. I do." she said. She would have hugged him if he was there. Maybe she would have given him a peck on his cheeks if she felt Barve.

"let's talk about something else" she said, to avoid going back to feeling vulnerable.

"what's your favorite movie?" she continued

"I don't have a favorite. There are a bunch of them."

"Guess what mine is?" she asked, thinking it's unusual for him to guess. Overconfidently she said "Fifty..."

"Fifty shades darker" Neel finished her sentence.

"How do you..."

"How do I know? You only told me "He finished her sentence again. I bet he had a smile lingering on his face. He knew she blacked out at Ruhan's party. He knew she would have forgotten what happened there.

"I saw you, all of you" he teased her. Her cheeks flushed. Heart raced. She had no memory of telling him any of it.

"Wait! When? Why do I not remember it?" she said. Being embarrassed.

"Not only tell, but you also did the actions as well." he teased more, "That too under a table away from the prying eyes"

Blurred mcmories of Ruhan's party appeared like a retro film. She remembered going under the table. What else did she do? What does he mean by actions? Did he use his hands or hers? Thoughts like this created cloud over her head. She felt exposed. The feelings that she tries hard not to show in front of Neel were out loud. And she can't blame anyone.

"Uh..." Paloma fought very hard to construct a sentence "Did I use. your hands or mine to explain the scene"

"Did Christian do it with his own hands?" Neel counter questioned.

The room was so silent that she could hear the cigarette burning. She couldn't utter a word. She tried. In her head. Her articulation skills did not support her. Did she make it awkward for him?

"Did you feel bad when I did what I did?" she pushed herself hard to speak.

"Why do you think so?" Neel said diplomatically.

"I think I needed you consent to do such a thing" Paloma spoke with a conscious tone.

"What have to done to me Paloma? Who will marry me now? I am not pure anymore." He tried to calm her down with sarcasm.

"You should sleep now. We have football tomorrow. See you in data structure class" he said before disconnecting.

He knows from the day one how she felt about him. The harder she tried to hide, the more obvious it was to him.

But for Neel, he has never seen a girl like paloma. He could talk to her about anything, anyone... no fear of judgements. She was most certainly not the most beautiful girl. But the way she smiled at silly things, made him laugh. The way she celebrated after scoring a goal made him excited. The innocent parts of her keep his innocence alive.

Neel was a guy who always danced between morals and desire. Neel's upbringing was firmly rooted in family values. His mom, like any typical mother, was both strict and caring, quick to scold her child but fiercely protective. His father, however, had unwavering faith in him, and his eyes beamed with pride whenever they met. Their family was like any other, built on a foundation of love.

Yet, Neel's childhood carried its own set of challenges. He grappled with insecurities as an overweight child. It wasn't until his first heartbreak that he decided to join the gym, marking the start of his transformation. Over time, he discovered a newfound confidence and charm he never knew he had.

11.30. Data structure class. The room hummed with inattentive students. Paloma, trying to keep her distance from Neel after last night, after her cover's blown, sat far from him.

Neel, however, playfully moved closer, taking a seat right behind her, unnoticed. Like a silent intruder,

"Hi" Neel whispered in her ears. From the seat behind. She gasped. Her pen slipped from her grasp and clattering onto her desk. Neel leaned back with a grin. He knew she was embarrassed being exposed. He wanted to have a little fun.

The entire day the series of "Hi"s continued. Every time he did that, she turned crimson. The signature smell of white-chocolate and Burbon makes her pulse quicken.

It was not fun. She was on a verge of letting go. Letting go of the guilt and shame for feeling whatever she felt for him. She felt like he wanted her to let go.

Once, while sharing a smoke that day at Ruhan's place, In the dimly lit room, the five of them lounged on a bed

Ruhan, positioned in the farthest corner of the bed said "Pass me the joint bro"

To pass the joint, Neel had to reach over Paloma, their bodies coming intimately close. It almost felt like he was on top of her, her heart longing for a kiss, their lips very dargerously close, separated by only a whisper of air.

He softly ran his fingers through her hair, aiming to playfully say "Hi" in her ears Paloma instinctively grasped his T-shirt, her breath hitching. His warm breath on her ear sent pleasant shivers down her spine.

Was it right? Or her part? To feel like this? On his part to make her feel like this? Who am I to judge?

Society tries to fit us in boxes. They are parents, they are to react in a certain way. They are committed, this should be their ideal behavior. These are the rules for friends. Sometimes I wonder, who created these rules? Was it created by a single man/woman? Or a committee? Why do we label someone who is different? I don't have answers to this.

A threshold is a boundary that, when reached and surpassed, results in dramatically new conditions. Sometimes, thresholds are referred to as "tipping points".

Threshold or not, what I know is, a portal has opened. A magical portal, and there stand two people. Two very vulnerable and different people. One step into this, and things are going to change dramatically.

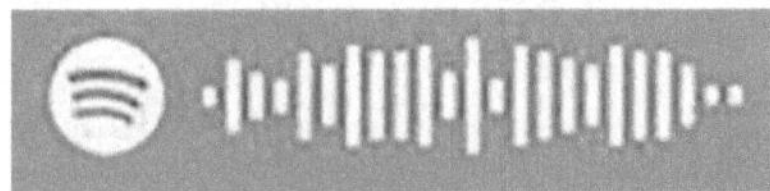

Chapter 9

DO YOU WANNA FEEL LIKE THIS?

"I can't do this, Paloma," Neel confessed, frustration evident in his voice. "Not to him, not to you... I just can't."

"Please, don't say that. We're already here," she defended herself.

"You know, you and I can't really happen. But you still chose to cheat!" He turned his gaze away, and it felt like an accusation, causing her heart to sink.

"Why are you having second thoughts? You know how I feel about you," Paloma pleaded, gently cupping his face in an attempt to convince him.

"Do you love him?" Neel asked, his gaze locked onto hers.

Paloma, her voice tinged with desperation, admitted, "I felt the same way when you were with Nazia. I shouldn't be the other girl."

"Is it a yes or no, Paloma?" Neel pressed.

Paloma hesitated before replying, "I think I do."

Neel looked down. "Then I'm that other guy," he muttered.

"You're my best friend!" Paloma exclaimed, gripping his hands tightly.

Neel sighed, his voice filled with conflict. "That makes it even more difficult. I'm supposed to be there for your worst moments, not be the cause."

He stood up, as if to leave the room, but Paloma pleaded, "Please, don't go."

"Dude, I love you," Neel said with a heavy heart. "I'm sorry I had to do this to you. I know you won't understand today. But someday you will."

He grabbed his jacket and quietly left the room, leaving Paloma behind in a whirlwind of emotions.

Pin-drop silence. Room smelling like nicotine. White bed sheets. White blankets. White pillows.

Paloma had always wondered how it felt to be numb. Was it a stage of feeling absolutely nothing? How could one truly feel like nothing? And then, that day, it happened to her. Tears didn't come, and she felt like a fraud, as if her emotions had abandoned her.

Why did he agree? Why did he show up? Why did he even care? These questions swirled in her mind, driving her to the brink of madness. She reached for the joint, its flames as fiery as her bleeding heart.

But what were they doing in that hotel room? The thing that two non-teenagers can do in an hourly rented hotel room. But perhaps the more intriguing question is, how did they end up there in the first place?

Football. Whiskey. Friends. Late night conversations.

This became the definition of paloma's life for the next 1 year. Paloma and Neel came closer, the attraction grew. Despite of her relationship and his failed attempts of love with Tuhina and Samantha, they became the only constant of each other's life.

Well, Neel had his own stuff going on too. Love showed up and took chunks out of him. Every time love didn't work out, it felt like a piece of him got chipped away. After a while, believing in love felt like chasing after a rainbow's end.

Satya on the other hand, did not take the changes gracefully. He felt secure if she spent time with HIS friends. It was frightening for Satya to accept that someone other than him someone could take care of Paloma. He felt betrayed by destiny because he knew sympathy was the only thing that bound them together, more than love.

Satya started feeling like sand slipping through his fingers whenever Paloma went off with her friends. He clung tighter, but it made things slip away even more.

With Mr. Insecure Boyfriend in the picture, the idea of "love at first sight" started to look even more appealing.

It could have been the simplest love story with these two vulnerable, hungry for love young college sweethearts. But Paloma's insecurities did not help. She always thought Neel was way out of her league. The body image issues she left unattended after Satya came to her life began to resurface and play a silent role in their story.

The tension became too much. The tug and war between the secure sympathetic future with Satya and hopeless love for Neel, she chooses the easy way out. Her heart yearned for Neel so as her body. If she leaves the lifeboat to chase the ship she might or might not make it. But the fear of floating in the ocean alone felt like a nightmare. She thought that the perfect plan would be chasing the ship in a life boat. That way she can find out if Neel feels the same about her, not wrecking her relationship completely with Satya. A mistake that could be forgiven.

One vulnerable night, when both of them were drunk, she said it all...

"I think I am attracted towards you." Paloma's message typed itself out, bravely.

"Do you think I don't know that" Neel's response was quick, tinged with playful confidence.

"I don't know if that's right" said paloma

"Right or wrong is relative" Neel expressed diplomatically

"I kind of know you don't feel the same" is she playing the damsel and distressed, or she was the one? hard to tell.

"I won't lie I have thought about it too" Neel stated in a moment of weakness

"I know I don't come close to the woman in your life, Tuhina, Samantha or Nazia... they are different, probably better" Paloma's doubts crept in.

"No one is comparing, besides confidence is sexy" he said convincingly

"Do you feel the same right now? Like if you were here, I couldn't hold myself back" paloma confessed

She closed her eyes, feeling a teasing tingle around her belly. All she could imagine was his lips .

Those lips that made her heart race.

The bright red lights only added to the excitement.

"Yeah? What would you like to do?" he pressed. She read the text from the notification bar. It hit her like a flogger, skillfully placed with a swing. Firm but playful.

She couldn't text back, she doesn't know. Maybe she would kiss his lips, maybe bite as well. Maybe the warmth of his breath will make her shiver. Maybe he would hold his hands to restrain her a little, maybe she would feel his lips on her neck and then different contours of her body. Maybe he would rip off her camisole, only to find her naked underneath.

The idea of her being naked, scared her a little. What-if he doesn't like what's underneath? What-if her scars were disgusting. What-if he thinks she is nasty. Not attractive at all. Her insecurities crawled up like zombies.

"What if I say I wanna kiss you right now?" Paloma's text appeared on Neel's screen, her words filled with longing.

"I wouldn't mind," Neel replied, a mischievous twinkle in his eye.

The flames of desire began to flicker higher as Paloma's next message appeared. "What if I say I want more than just kissing? What if I want to kiss your neck?"

Neel's heart skipped a beat as he read her words. "All over me?"

A playful smile tugged at Paloma's lips as she typed, "I would love to."

Neel's mind raced, his imagination running wild. "Maybe I would lick you."

Paloma's breath hitched, her fingers trembling slightly. "I would grab your hair."

Neel's thoughts became bolder, his words dripping with desire. "I would slap you down there with my thing. And make you beg to put it in."

Paloma gasped, her body shivering with anticipation. "Ohhhh dear god. I would die for it."

A smirk played at the corners of Neel's mouth as he responded, "I won't let you die. But you would want to"

Paloma's voice trembled as she typed, "Give it to me." Neel's eyes gleamed with dominance. "Beg for it."

"Please..." Paloma pleaded, her voice barely a whisper.

"Please what?" Neel teased, relishing in her desperation.

"I would say please put it in," Paloma confessed, her desire laid bare. Neel's pulse quickened, his voice filled with command. "Put what in?"

Paloma's response was breathless and raw. "Your dick."

Neel's fingers hovered over the keys, teasing her further. "Where do you want it?"

"In my pussy, baby," Paloma's text oozed with need. A wicked grin spread across Neel's face. "You would have to say please."

Paloma's heart raced as she complied, her words laced with longing. "Please do it, and don't stop."

"I won't," Neel promised, his voice dripping with desire. "Even if you ask me to. I'll take you from the back."

A gasp escaped Paloma's lips. "And fuck me hard?" Her words were filled with primal hunger.

"I'm just getting started. I'll grab your arms from the back. And push it even harder" he said

"Oh, this is like a dream!" she texted

"Put your fingers inside you now. And feel it" he instructed.

Paloma felt something different that day. She felt like a different person. She hasn't felt happiness like this before. Her body, her mind, her heart all in sink.

Their charm lay in their anticipation of the first time. It was all within their minds, They imagined each other time and time again in their heads. Their imaginations ran wild. Rough. They spoke about it many times after that night.

Have you ever seen addicts in the real world? Like the ones hooked on pills? After a while, if they don't get their fix, their bodies react. Well Paloma's body started reacting. Her body is not satisfied with the doses of virtual encounters. She needed more, they needed more.

The excitement of intimacy made her heart ache a little less but with each passing day, it became more difficult to not fall for Neel. Sometimes she traded the exclusivity she craved with him, for the desires piling up inside her. Neel tried warning her. But what's the meaning of re-considering when you already shot someone. Better you make a team and start hiding the body. That's what she thought. But Neel knew the consequences. he has been on both sides. He knew either way it's not getting a fairytale ending. But he also knew it was too late.

He loved her, in his own unique manner. He cared for her, in his own distinctive style. Expressing emotions wasn't his strong suit and he did not try. He behaved differently when they were around people, worrying if what they had, got out in public, she would be in trouble. He hated the feeling of being a homewrecker. Paloma misunderstood his feelings. She took in with a pinch of salt. She always thought feelings were one sided. Her insecurities drove Neel away sometimes. But he couldn't hate her. I believe he loved her. Every time he was rude to her, and she cared, he loved her a little more every time.

It's mesmerizing how two people, on complete two different phases of their lives, choose to float together for a while. The freshly heartbroken prince charming was taken by his desires when paloma asked to spend a night together. A night when finally, they could tear down the virtual wall between them. A getaway from the boundaries of the societal morals which she had to follow.

In the end Morals: 1 desires: 0.5 that's what the scoreline was. A tale of pleasure and thin lines. Win? Or loss? It makes no difference. Until next time...

Chapter 10

KNOCK KNOCK... WHO'S THERE!

Water pouring from an expensive shower head. Noise of water. Smell of alcohol and nasty food. Hands clasping ears. And all she could hear was an undertone of an elongated beep sound.

She feels dirty. She feels filthy. She rolls up the sleeves of the soaked hoodie and tries to clean herself. Nothing comes off… the stains ran much deeper than water could reach.

Last night, their college hosted a fresher's party for their juniors. It was a big event. And guess what? The spotlight was on Paloma and Somali! They had recently bagged victory in the inter-college futsal tournament, and tonight was the night they would proudly receive their well-deserved trophy. Imagine the thrill of stepping onto that stage, eyes on them, applause echoing in their ears, It was a scene they were quite familiar with, having secured the championship for the past three consecutive years. It had become an annual tradition.

Paloma decided she wants to wear her off shoulder dress. A pink maxi dress revealing just enough to stroke desires. Satya, however, was not very happy with the decision. He never wanted paloma to wear a revealing dress when he was not around. But unlike before, today she wanted to feel sexy, embrace her body. But we all knew paloma was very insecure about her body. An interesting how…

Ever heard of the 'like attract like' theory? Well according to Helena Blavatsky, the inventor of 'law of attraction',

Atoms that have energy and are drawn towards atoms with similar energy composition. The law of attraction states that thoughts are like atoms, drawn towards similar kind of thoughts.

Even after what went down in that cheap hotel room between Paloma and prince charming, like attracted like. Neel and Paloma prioritized their friendship over the social dilemma.

Even though they managed to come out alive with a moral score from that hotel room, it was not that easy to stop what they started. The visuals, snapshots, and even some steamy videos kept the fire burning.

Initially Paloma was unsure about stripping down and posing for the camera, it felt as comfortable as shoes, a size too small.

Satya's desires were easy to satisfy – he hungered for images that were as direct as a punch to the gut. Cropped shots of her breasts or down there, no frills, no fuss. It was as if his patience was wearing thin, instant gratification without the need for elaborate setups or artful poses.

But Neel wanted to wrap her breasts in lovely lingerie, he believed not showing is sexier than showing. No cropping this time, he yearned to see her lips, her collarbone, her eyes... He wished for her to enjoy her own body, to grab every curve with passion. Every smile, every shape, he wanted her to love it all, and his appreciation became her potion of confidence, a daily sip of empowerment. With each passing day, she became a lot more confident than before, ignited by his gaze and ignited by his words.

It felt oddly familiar to the audio drama they couldn't get enough of, 'Bondhu Biday'. Picture this: in the drama, a guy and a girl shared a kiss at a college fest while Fossils' "Hasnuhana" played in the background. Paloma's college did not have the budget for fossils, but the cheap Dj and enough booze to give the feel of it.

"You look... different..." Neel said, looking into paloma's eyes when no one looked at them.

"I wanted to dress up, I feel different" paloma stared right back at those beautiful eyes.

"I would probably kiss you if no one was here" he confessed, his fingers gently grazing her hair.

She pressed her lips together and looked up at him. Her skin is hot like fire. No one can tell if it's the Rum they were drinking or him.

She gulped the alcohol, without water, to numb her instincts. Poor child, she doesn't know, alcohol dominates and heightens people's impulses.

"Don't drink too much, you know what happens after that." Neel carefully took away the glass from her hand. Fingers touched. Electrical touch. Paloma was just soaking everything; she couldn't say anything.

"The moment I saw you, on the stage... something inside me wanted to rip the dress apart..." Neel confessed. He was pretty drunk as well, otherwise he is not the 'sharing what I felt' type

Paloma's breath caught in her throat, her eyes fluttering closed. The moonlight draped her in a warm, crimson glow, painting her cheeks and collarbone with liquid silver. Neel's gaze traced the path from her eyes to her flushed cheeks and down to her lips.

It's almost like she is the submissive, who is bound to a seat. Her master gets to tickle, spank, and gently tug, while she's under strict "no noise" orders. It's all a thrilling game where even a peep could mean game over! The mental bondage, a tango of power and submission, sends ripples of excitement through her. As her mind succumbs to the thrill, her body responds, aching with a delicious tension. Each thought, each suggestion, pulls her deeper into a realm of arousal, leaving her, well, wet with anticipation.

"Please... either kiss me or stop this..." Paloma implored, her thighs pressed together, aching for fulfillment.

"I would love to, see how you taste like..." Neel whispered, his voice thick with desire.

"You know what I would like to do?" Paloma's voice firm as she spoke. Enough teasing, she thought.

"Imagine me giving you a nice massage," Paloma's words flowed, a sultry tone lacing her voice.

"Yeah...I'd like that," Neel's response held a hint of desire.

"Wearing nothing, or anything you would like," she added, the anticipation thickening the air between them.

"Nothing sounds better," Neel whispered.

"Nothing it is," Paloma replied with a seductive smile.

"Exploring the contours of you..." she said while exploring the crock of his neck with her forefinger. A gentle touch to tickle his soul a little. Taste of his own medicine, after all she learned from the best

"Licking you, like my favorite treat, exploring every inch, with wet kisses." Paloma whispered,

This is the kind of confidence that pushes all of Neel's buttons. The prince charming was about to kiss Cinderella, but the spell broke. Midnight struck her in the form of a phone call. Neel saw the name of the person when paloma was taking out her phone from the purse. Satya.

"Pass me the joint bro" Neel said, giving Paloma a slight nod, his eyes carrying a mixture of emotions. He then joined Samarth, who was already enjoying a smoke.

She did not pick up. she did not pick up his call. The phone never stopped buzzing. she felt like someone with a strike of knife cut through her wings.

The next morning when she came home. When the Dj stopped playing, when alcohol wore her off, when her friends went home, that is when she needed Satya. This was a marriage of convenience.

Firstly, she wore the dress he did not approve of, secondly, she did not follow the curfew time set by him, and lastly, she did not pick up his calls, Paloma knew what awaited her. When she called Satya back the next day, he behaved like an angry brown father. After an hour of telephonic 'to and fro' they thought it best to resolve this in person.

Imagine this, a tiny room. No windows. A tv that has only two channels. News playing. Diplomats fighting over petty issues. Anyone would get tired of fighting after an hour. They gave each other a little break.

As the night progressed, Satya approached Paloma. Paloma knew the meaning of meeting him in a hotel room. she thought if having sex could fix their problem, she'd do it over and over. Maybe she'd enjoy it a little few time as well.

Paloma did not stop Satya though he smelled like cheap alcohol and was not in his senses. Satya did not like foreplay that much, just like his virtual desires, he wanted things to be direct. three things. breasts, vagina and I started the sentence as if there were a third thing. but she never complained. He is the only one she did it with. So, she thinks this is how it's done. poor child...

but tonight is a little different. He did not want to do anything with her breasts. Generally, that's where he starts. He did not care if she was wet or not, he dragged her pants down, and pushed himself in with friction. In a state of complete dismay her mind raced to thoughts like,

"*Is he angry? Frustrated? Drunk? Whatever it is, let's get over it with quickly,*" she thought.

With her head constantly thudding against the bedpost, she tried desperately to block her uneasiness. "*Maybe this is his way of showing love,*" she contemplated to herself.

"*Is it because I mentioned BDSM that he's trying to assert his dominance?*" thoughts weaving through her mind as she stared into the blank.

he clawed her neck, and with every thrust he said

"Neel, your best friend wants to fuck you like this, Ruhan your friend wants to bang you like this, who's left... yeah Samarth he wants to fuck you like this. I know you wanna take all of them you whore."

This continued for the next ten minutes... until he was done. she didn't have the courage to push him. a flashback of feelings bound her numb to the bed. This was not the first time, well first time with Satya...

She stood under the shower for an hour with her clothes on, unable to understand whether she should cry, is this her fault?

Love is not confusing. Love never drags you down. Love never makes you feel shitty about yourself. Love teaches you empathy. Love teaches you respect. Love never hits you, love asks for consent. She should have pushed him, got out of the room, asked for help. She did not. We all have gone through the same at some point of our lives, we choose to give another person a benefit of doubt. Do we ask ourselves, "*do they deserve the chance?*" or next morning like Satya they gonna wake up with a hangover just to say

"Hey... I was drunk, and I told you not to make me angry. You chose to make me angry by going out with your friends, you brought it on yourself" with no remorse in his tone.

Is it okay, to be shattered from inside for someone, anyone? Why did she not have the courage to break free from this? Why does she suffer from these insecurities like "what if no one likes me?" Well biggest question was why didn't she like herself?

The blame in a relationship often falls on the one, who cheats or deceives, and rightly so.

The silent burden of carrying your own secrets remains unseen. Paloma, deep in her heart, carried the weight of guilt, believing she was inherently bad and deserved the torment she endured. This internal struggle kept her silent, unwilling to confide in anyone. On the other hand, Satya, with his narcissistic tendencies, thought he could blame it on alcohol and her and get away with this.

But she felt the pain distinctively when she got the news that after the fresher's party Neel got a text from Nazia, she said sorry for pushing Neel away, one thing led to another, and they decided to meet.

The only person Paloma thought of, seeking refuge, who can put her mind to rest, is gone. The one that makes her feel safe. The one who has seen her naked mind and did not judge, the one she can think out loud with. She lost everything that one night, the feeling of a safe space with Satya and the love of her life Neel.

She tried, she tried not to feel the pain she felt. She reminded herself of the choice that she made a while ago.

She chose her desires over her heart. But now she felt complicated. Unseen. Unwanted.

Unaware that she is the one making it complicated for herself...

"let's drink" is what she said to Ruhan on a phone call.

"Cool, I will call Smail (Somali), she also wanted to sit. I don't think Neel will come today, and Samarth did not pick up my call" Ruhan replied from the other end.

"I haven't ate anything from last night, grab some food"

"Come!" Ruhan reassured "Hey Palo? Are you all, right?" he asked, he knew she would be upset.

"Like a charm! Be there in fifteen minutes" paloma tried hard to maintain her act of 'nothing happened'

They met after an hour, she tried her best to cover her puffy eyes with concealer. Somali bought a plus one. She has been dating this guy for a while now.

They started drinking following the house rules. First drink, 60ml, raw. As paloma said on call, she did not eat anything since last night, and today neither Neel nor Samarth was there to regulate the pegs. She started drinking raw from the bottle.

Next thing you know, she has her phone in hand with a bunch of drunk messages.

4:32 PM - Paloma: I just wanted to tell you; you are a... The good guy... guy... You are not like the other guy... You are the good guy... I want to break up... With Satya. Please take me... Can you? I will never make you feel unwanted. Am I not pretty to you? I wanted to be with you. It's not all sexual...

As the night progressed, the volume of alcohol was inversely proportional to the coherence of her texts. Her phone became her canvas, and her thumbs danced drunkenly over the keyboard, painting a masterpiece of intoxicated communication. In this chaos, parts of her thoughts appeared like hidden treasures in a scavenger hunt. The texts morphed into an emotional rollercoaster, swinging between comedic misspellings and genuine vulnerability.

After a point Neel stopped replying. Why I can understand. Paloma is putting him in a difficult position. Nazia is Neel's one true love. And she knew that. His heart ached for her. And she knew that. He mentioned a million times, how much it hurt him when she left him. And finally, when she was around, when they got a fair shot, Paloma behaved like a child. A child who is not willing to let go. Obviously, Neel did not knew about last night like we do. Imagine if we found Paloma's behavior a little off the hook, how did he feel? He cannot take the chance. Everyone vs Nazia, Neel would chose her. A million times. And Paloma knew that,

Why did she take her chances at the worst possible time? Was she looking for her home? A person who understood her the best? A person who can clean those stains. A person who would say, "Don't bring him in front of me, I would punch him in his face" she wanted someone else to fight her battles. How is that fair? Is it the end of them?

When she came home, the tipsiness went away. She doesn't remember how her girl-friend's lips met those of the new guy – was he, her boyfriend? She forgot how Ruhan, with all his heart, took care of her when she puked, On his clothes. Only thing she remembers is how Neel did not reply. She couldn't sleep that night. She couldn't let this end. Not like this...

Sound of a door bell. Nervous nail biting. "who's there" of an Indian vigilant mom from the other side. Moments of silence. Thud of a door lock.

"Holy fuck!" Neel gasped

Infront of him, stands paloma.

She couldn't let go. She was not able to.

"Before you ask me to go away, hear me out" paloma requested with teary eyes. She was so sure that Neel was going to shoo her away.

"Come in you idiot!" Neel said, with mixed emotions.

Remember, when I told you, Neel loved Paloma a little more when he pushed her away and she cared. Maybe he liked the fact that, someone is ready to fight for him, against anything. Someone chooses him over anyone, every time.

"You look... horrible." Neel tried not to care, but he did.

"I'm an idiot," Paloma admitted, regret weighing down her words. "I shouldn't have acted like that."

"I can't agree more." Neel's tone was rude, but his heart melted.

"Will you forgive me? Can we go back to being friends? I cannot lose you." paloma pleaded.

"Ma... Paloma's here, I don't know why... mind taking out an extra plate for her" Neel shouted.

"I'll leave..." paloma hesitated

"Sit!" Neel said, giving her a side-eye.

During that precious half-hour lunch, all of Paloma's problems seemed to vanish. Neel's parents had this magical way of making her feel right at home. Laughter echoed around the table as they shared jokes and stories. Paloma couldn't help but grin at Neel's mom when she playfully scolded her for not eating her veggies – a scene straight out of her own mom's playbook. The aroma of the homemade khichdi filled the air, wrapping them all in a comforting embrace. In those simple moments, surrounded by good food, loving company, and genuine care, Paloma found a slice of solace that felt just like home.

"Why do you drink like this?" Neel asked post lunch.

"Because I am stupid." She tried to act normal, "Leave my problems... you look happy."

Neel did not reply understanding where this conversation was going, and he already knew how it would make Paloma feel. Paloma got the hint that he needed an explanation. She hesitated for a second, to share about the horrible night.

Telling him about it would make her relive the night. She is not sure if she is able to do that or not.

"Satya and I... we kinda had a rough night, post fresher's party" Paloma confessed.

"What do you mean by rough night?" Neel asked.

Paloma told Neel what happened, she had to let it out of her chest. She tried to defend Satya as much as possible, with her wrong doings, with her being the bad person. Paloma tried justifying Satya's actions by bringing in a Karma-angle.

Did Neel's heart sink a little? Did his skin burn, with anger? Did he feel like kissing her? Did he feel like comforting her a little?

He just stared at her, not knowing how to maybe.

Chapter 11

OH FUCK! WHY AM I DRESSED!

A single bed. Soft morning glow. Goan sunlight filtering through sheer curtains. Sound of ocean. Paloma slowly stirs, her eyelids fluttering open.

She is not alone... Neel is beside her, "the fuck! Why am I fully dressed?" was her first thought when she lifted the blanket

He is still asleep, appears peaceful and unaware. His chest rises and falls rhythmically as he breathes.

Neel's fingers twitch slightly, and then his hand moves, reaching out for Paloma. It lands gently on her waist, and he unconsciously pulls her closer. Neel nuzzles his face into the crook of Paloma's neck, his grip on her tightening ever so slightly. It's as if he's seeking comfort in her presence.

Is she dreaming? If yes, she doesn't wanna get up.

Wait, Lemme explain...

She did not understand the degree of abuse, mental and sexual. She continued her strings with Satya carrying the burden of being the villain. Satya unapologetically continued his existence.

In the midst of twisted truths and careful cover-ups, Paloma found herself stuck. Being honest didn't help her situation, so she decided that Satya shouldn't know about her close-knit group. She thought it was for his own good. Now, she had to figure out how to spend time with her friends without making Satya aware.

Easier said than done, of course.

And so began the secret journey of managing two WhatsApp accounts, deleting photos, chats, and call records. Why, you ask? Well, if you've ever been in a relationship like this, you know that the password becomes synonymous with trust. It's all part of the delicate dance of hiding her life from Satya, a dance she was becoming quite skilled at. Unknowingly Satya was giving birth to Paloma 2.0.

And to be honest, she grew up in a strict household, lies and deception have been in her since forever. It was not very difficult for her to download the fake location app, to deceive Satya if he asked for live locations.

From stolen kisses in the dark corners of the movie theater while watching the magnificence of "Bohemian Rhapsody," to surprising Nazia with her favorite dessert when she was feeling down, Neel had put in the effort. He had tried so damn hard.

But deep down he knew she was like a walking red flag. And if he dared to analyze their relationship, he couldn't help but notice the striking similarities between Nazia and Paloma.

Emotionally unstable, always making impulsive decisions, and never learning from their mistakes, both Nazia and Paloma were cut from the same wild cloth. The only difference was that Paloma wore her flaws proudly, while Nazia hid behind a facade of perfection.

Neel found himself torn between two women. Was he falling for both? Well, I don't know.

One evening after a football match,

"Let's plan something," Somali suggested, her voice budding with anticipation.

Ruhan, leaning back against a tree, chuckled. "Plan what? Every day is a plan at my place."

Paloma joined in, balancing the football on her knee.

"No, I mean, let's go on a trip." Somali specified.

Samarth's eyes lit up. "I'm thinking beach and booze!"

"Goa," Ruhan declared with a knowing smirk. Paloma said "Satya is in Delhi. So yes, from my side."

Neel, a hint of concern in his voice, kicked the ball back. "Are you sure? It won't cause any drama, right?"

Paloma swirled her foot around the ball, a determined smile on her lips. "Let's do it. I could use a vacation."

Samarth raised his hand in excitement. "Then it's settled! WE ARE GOING TO GOA!"

It was Paloma's chance to escape reality. Satya has been in Delhi for his new job for one week. She hatched the perfect plan to call in sick from her duty calls with him. Three days, no phone weekend... and he will never have to know about the trip.

Paloma, Somali, Ruhan, Samarth and Neel, along with two of their batchmates Yudh and Raj landed Goa.

They made their way to their accommodation, a cozy villa nestled in a serene part of Goa. It was a spacious and well-furnished place, complete with a private swimming pool and a breathtaking view of the beach. The excitement in the air was palpable as they settled into their new home for the next few days.

"Look what I got" Somali pointed out an alcohol bottle before going to the beach.

Neel Yudh and Raj were still changing. Paloma, Ruhan, Samarth and Somali took their turns and finished the bottle raw. While Samarth was relishing the last sip of it,

"What the fuck guys?" Neel said in surprise standing by the door,

They looked at each other and busted in laughter "Welcome to goa" all four of them screamed in chorus

With the taste of alcohol on their lips and excitement in their hearts, they stormed the beach like kids in a candy store. Laughter filled the air as they played tag, the palm trees swaying to their joy. The salty ocean splashes added to their delight. guys raced the waves, Somali and Paloma watched them.

"Here we are," Paloma said with a nervous smile.

Somali, her ever-observant friend, sensed something amiss. "Here we are... Did Satya call?"

Paloma hesitated for a moment before responding, "He did. But I texted that I'm sick, took some medicine, and I'm going to sleep."

Somali's eyes darted over to Neel, who seemed to be in high spirits. "Neel looks happy," she remarked.

Paloma forced a smile, masking her inner turmoil. "I'm happy for him."

Somali wasn't easily convinced. She prodded further, "So, you're sure nothing's going to happen? You keep telling me how much you love him."

Paloma sighed, her gaze still fixed on Neel, who looked incredibly appealing under the sun. His body looked even better than before. The water droplets on his skin made his muscles stand out. You could see his six-pack abs more clearly, and his chest and arms looked strong "I do, I still do. Look at him, he looks like a snack," she admitted, her desire palpable.

"Are you gonna join or not?" Ruhan shouted.

"Coming!" Paloma shouted back. She turned to Somali and said, "I don't wanna think about it. Let's have fun." Somali nodded

They ran around in the soft sand, the sun making their skin warm. Paloma acted like the ball in a game of catch, and everyone laughed a lot. Sometimes, Paloma jumped on Neel's back. Samarth noticed this and winked at Paloma whenever she did that, as if he was rooting for them.

Two days whizzed past with beach parties, football games, and boundless fun, making Paloma feel like she was living in a dream. For a little while, she nearly pushed her boyfriend and her life at home out of her thoughts.

the entire trip, she sat in the farthest corner from Neel, but she couldn't avoid those gorgeous eyes. It was like she knew he almost loved her, and so did she. But no one accepted. You talk to different people, you smile and have fun. But inside you wish there is a parallel universe where you can be together, sitting by each other. Looking into each other's eyes under the sun. The feeling never goes away. It just grew stronger. Inside both bodies, untill the bodies explode.

But this time she didn't want things to get awkward, especially during the trip, especially since Neel had already made amends with Nazia.

The last night, they decided to create a bonfire and sit around it. As the sun went down and the sky turned pretty colors, Paloma and her friends were having a fun time at the beach.

Samarth prepared a chillum and handed it over to Neel. He drew deeply from the chillum before extending it to Yudh. Eventually Ruhan passed it to Paloma. For a moment, she hesitated, "I'm not sure how to hold it," she confessed.

I am unsure what exactly happened inside Neel, but he got up and sat behind paloma, who was sitting cross-legged.

He spread both his arms arround her neck and held the chillam near her face.

"You have to hold the chillum between your thumb and forefinger. Your thumb should rest on the top, while your forefinger supports it from below."

Half of his face was lit with warm shades of the bonfire, while the other half of his face was dark. His warm breath on Paloma's neck, his word in her ears... heightened all her senses,

She couldn't help but wonder, "How would he taste like if I kiss him?" white chocolate with hazelnut, subtly tinged with the essence of burned wood.

Her lips, pressed together in contemplation, unaware that her subtle actions were not without consequences. Her nearness, the subtle scent of her skin, and the intimacy of the situation heightened his longing for her. He could feel his heart beating faster, his body responding to her presence in a way that was impossible to ignore.

"We have to change the teacher, Paloma is distracted with this one" Yudh shouted making both of them conscious.

Samarth couldn't help but notice the subtle change in Paloma's expression when Neel got up and returned to his place. Her attempt to conceal her disappointment was commendable. But Samarth knew her enough to read the situation.

Somali, accompanied by Ruhan, excused themselves and headed to the restroom. Yudh and Raj had concocted their alibis and slipped away from the noise and the bonfire to maintain the secrecy of their presence in Goa, hidden from their unsuspecting girlfriends. Meanwhile, Samarth had an excuse of his own. He claimed to want to enjoy the scenic beauty of the night sea and excused himself leaving Neel and Paloma sitting by the bonfire...

"Cheers!" was the first thing they said after a long silence. With him silence was comfortable. They smiled at each other. Looked into each other's eyes.

"How are things with Nazia?" Paloma asked,

Neel sighed, his shoulders slumping slightly. "Things are different. It's not like the first time, you know, when it was all roses and pink. I hate the fact that she still talks to Pratim, her ex... she says they are just friends."

Paloma nodded understandingly. "I'm sure you guys will figure it out. Relationships have their ups and downs."

"Yeah, I will," Neel replied, though his tone held a hint of uncertainty.

"You can talk to me about anything, Neel," Paloma said softly, her voice filled with warmth and sincerity. "I am and will always be here for you."

Despite the confusing and complex feelings they experienced, they remained each other's best friends first and foremost.

As the night progressed, Paloma continued to indulge in drinks until she was almost unable to walk on her own. Her words slurred as she murmured, "I wanna talk... I wanna walk in the beach and feel the wet sand in my toes"

She tried getting up, but was too dizzy, Neel scooped her up into his arms, her head resting gently on his shoulder. Paloma's arms wrapped loosely around his neck as she mumbled something incoherent.

Carrying her through the dimly lit villa, Neel moved through the hallways to Paloma's room. He gently placed her on the bed, tucking her in and ensuring she was comfortable. Her eyes fluttered, but she remained in a drunken stupor.

Just as Neel was about to quietly exit the room, Samarth's voice cut through the stillness. "Bro, Somali accidentally fell asleep in your bed, and everyone else is dozed off. Will you manage with Paloma tonight?"

Was that intentional what Samarth did? Who can tell?

Two drunk non-teenagers, who spoke about sleeping together all the time, who craved each other's skin all the time, slept under a blanket that day... did they kiss? Did they feel each other's skin, did they made love?

Well, we don't know, because they don't know.

Chapter 12

THE WEDDING

An exquisite lehenga, embroidered with delicate threads. shimmered under the warm light's radiance. His arms wrapped around her. Intricate patterns of the lehenga, pressed against his skin. Lips met. Waves of electricity. Surged through their bodies. Both tender and fierce. she tasted like a blend of strawberry and dark chocolate, both sweet and sinful. Their first kiss.

Neel was too careful to mess up Paloma's meticulously done hairdo, his fingertips gently caressing the intricate curls. They held each other tightly, their bodies burning with desire. Paloma's fingers entwined with Neel's

They broke apart momentarily, their breaths ragged, it felt not enough. They have waited for three years for this. When Paloma looked at Neel, in his beige sherwani, it felt like he had stepped out of her dreams, Unable to resist any longer, Neel pulled Paloma in for another kiss, this time with a hunger that had been building for far too long. Her body pressed against the rough wall. They were almost become one person. Neel's hands travelled down Paloma's back, the sensation of her soft skin driving him wild, with need. Paloma's hands explored Neel's strong shoulders, her touch sending shivers down his spine. The room was filled with moans and gasps, drowning out any doubts or fears that had lingered between them.

They lost track of time and the thought of their partners, Satya and Nazia, faded into the distance as the undeniable connection between them took center stage.

Why were they dressed in traditional clothing? It was Somali's elder sister's wedding. The wedding they have planned about, since the beginning of time. But after all this that's the question you want to ask?

When she came back from the trip and switched her phone back on. For three days, no calls, no messages. She couldn't catch up with the lies and calling in sick. She got busy living her life. When Satya found out, Paloma was in Goa, the intensity of calling and texting increased exponentially. "The number you are trying to reach is other switched of or out of network area. Please call back after some time" was the only reply that he could hear.

"Where were you?" Satya asked calmly to create authority. when she finally picked up the call.

"Goa" Paloma reciprocated even more calmly and dropped the bomb.

"You are kidding. You don't have the guts" Satya said sarcastically.

"Okay..." Paloma replied

"What do you mean you went to Goa?" This time Satya stammered.

"I mean to say I went to Goa with my friends" Paloma replied sternly.

"Which friends?" Satya asked frantically.

"The one's you hate..." Paloma replied with confidence.

After that, the conversation became more of a manchild crying and using curse words at the same time, His efforts to control and manipulate the situation, akin to the ringmaster's whip cracking and commands was not working anymore.

"I can't do this anymore. Not when you are cheating on me" Satya made it clear.

“I am not cheating on you, I am living my life” Paloma defended herself.

“Listen, shut the fuck up, don’t play this game with me, if you were so confident that you are not cheating, why did you hide this from me” Satya countered.

“Because you wouldn’t understand. You would make sure I didn’t go. Made me feel guilty for wanting to go” Paloma stated the facts.

Satya’s voice grew fervent, each word carrying the weight of his sacrifices. “Do you know what I’ve done for you? For those morning breakfasts, I skipped my own. To give you those expensive gifts I have not bought anything for myself, to bring you back home, I have waited for to five hours outside your college.”

Tears welled up in Paloma’s eyes, her voice quivering as she realized the chasm between them. “But... you see, it’s not about the sacrifices you’ve made. It’s about the freedom I’ve lost, the dreams I’ve abandoned. You’ve become my father, not my partner, and that’s the pain you don’t seem to grasp.”

Every conversation... each time Satya tried to control her...every small soft manipulation flashed before her eyes. It was as though a veil had been lifted, exposing the naked truth of Satya’s intentions, and the ugliness within became starkly evident.

“You have left me no choice. You have to decide Paloma... You want your friends, or you want to be with me...” his voice firm as a feminist’s beliefs.

“Well see, see? This is what I am talking about. You just try to control me, what if I want both, as you and my friends hold a different place in my heart” Paloma yelled with frustration.

“Then you choose them. I don’t want a partner who doesn’t value my opinion” Satya gave an ultimatum.

Was it that easy to decide? Why we have to choose? Specially us women? Between friends and boyfriend? Between Carrer and family? Between love and desire? Why is it wrong to want to have everything?

You know what was wrong? Putting herself in a situation where she has to lie. Not communicating her needs from the beginning. Letting go of herself to satisfy someone else’s needs. Pushing her limits until she can’t.

She suddenly remembers how it all started. When Paloma and Satya started dating, and she lied to him, about not masturbating. She thought if he knew she touched herself maybe he would think differently about her. When she told him, he was the first man, who touched her, and he was not. But she did not know how to explain, her first time with a man was forced. The seventeen year old Paloma did not know how to share, the first time, she had feelings for someone, and called her in her home and the man pushed her mouth down his genitals and made her feel dirty. She thought maybe he would think she was dirty. She remembered how she did not tell him that, with utter desperation of being seen, how she sent her nudes to a much older director way before they came in a relationship. All these lies started way before Neel came to her life. Now that she is thinking about it, she couldn't remember one single reason why she claims she loves Satya.

Do we be in a relationship with people sometimes because it's so scary being alone? Do we sacrifice our mental peace just to come home to a known face? Why do we limit ourselves?

Well to answer the main question, she did not choose. But someone once said "I can always choose, but I ought to know that if I do not choose, I am still choosing.". she chooses not to choose.

She behaves like a perfect girlfriend in front of Satya and his friends. Now that Satya is in Delhi, his friends behaved like her local guardian. Over and above, Paloma has proved she 'had the guts' to pull off something like Goa, the security had to become tighter. But it was a cake walk for paloma to escape every now and then in a long-distance relationship.

And now that Neel is busy with Nazia, the only thing she focused on was her friends, so she did not feel the guilt of lying anymore.

One day, she took Ruhan to the Academy of Fine Arts. For hours they looked at mesmerizing art, drank tea, smoked cigarettes. At the end of the day, they sat by the water, when the sun began to set casting an amber glow on the St. Paul's cathedral on the other side. They sat in silence and watched the indo-gothic architecture of the church vanish in the dark.

The other day, paloma and Somali put out their own tent in Ruhan's balcony, went inside in a rainy day sat there and watched Friends on Netflix.

Because of Satya, she couldn't post any of these on social media. It turned up to be a blessing in disguise for her. She did not click pictures of those moments, she lived them, she felt them.

As the calendar pages turned, March slowly transformed into September. Amidst all the life drama, it was that time of the year when college campus placements took center stage. This was the season when even the coolest kids didn't seem cool at all. The usually bustling football grounds now lay deserted, and the college uniforms remained untouched.

However, unlike most students, Paloma didn't need anyone to remind her of her reality. She was acutely aware of how she had passed those exams and the depth of her knowledge. As a result, she made a deliberate choice not to participate in the placement drive.

Neel's patience wore thin as he watched Paloma flip through the placement brochure for the umpteenth time, her anxiety growing palpable. He cleared his throat and said sternly, "Paloma, I've tried to be patient, but this is getting ridiculous."

Paloma looked up, her brow furrowing. "What's ridiculous?"

"You!" Neel snapped. "You're being utterly ridiculous by not even trying. Look at you, worrying about your grades and not even giving it a shot."

"Come on, Paloma. Today's the day we tackle this head-on," Neel said, standing up

Paloma sighed, "It's not that simple, Neel. I have terrible grades, no internships, and no idea how to answer those interview questions."

Neel, though frustrated, softened his tone a bit. "Look, Paloma, I get it. But you can't hide forever. Trust me"

He took her hand gently and led her towards the placement cell. There, he grabbed an application form and handed it to Paloma. "Fill it, now," he directed firmly.

Paloma looked at him, uncertainty in her eyes. Neel raised his eyebrows and pointed his fingers towards the application

It was weirdly satisfying, watching Neel support Paloma not only in the emotional ventures of her life but practically as well.

As they were heading out of the placement cell, they ran into Somali, who appeared to be quite excited. She waved them over, saying, "Guys, I need to tell you something!"

She had to be excited, her only sister was getting married. And the gang have been planning for this their entire college life.

"November 19th! That's just next month. Have we decided on our outfits?" Paloma chimed in.

Somali didn't hold back, saying, "We're going all out with yellow for the haldi ceremony. I won't tolerate any deviations."

Neel couldn't resist adding, "Make sure Samarth gets the memo."

As they wrapped up their conversation, they seamlessly merged into the bustling crowd. It was like they became one with the ebb and flow of the campus, blending into a sea of students. The chatter of countless voices filled the air, each voice a storyteller in their own right.

You could hear the laughter of friends sharing jokes, the earnest discussions of study groups preparing for placements, and the excited plans of those organizing events. Every step in this lively campus seemed to come with a snippet of a story, a glimpse into someone's world.

A week passes, and the college campus remains a hub of activity. Students bustle about, their voices blending into a cacophony of anticipation and excitement. The placement drive is just around the corner, and tension simmers beneath the surface.

Paloma, feeling a little nervous but determined, walked into the room for her first job interview. The person who was going to decide if she got the job looked grumpy and unfriendly. This job was in sales, which meant she had to persuade people to buy things, and she knew it wouldn't be easy. Still, she tried to stay calm and confident as she sat down.

At one point, she couldn't help but smile politely as she answered a particularly tricky question. The interviewer, noticing her smile, paused and asked in a rather sarcastic tone, "What's so funny? Am I telling you a joke?"

It was a test, a way to see if Paloma could handle pressure and maintain her composure even when faced with a somewhat rude remark. Paloma, though taken aback for a moment, kept her smile intact and replied with grace, "No, not at all. I just believe that a positive attitude can make any situation better."

Fast forward to a different day, a day filled with excitement and joy. It was Somali's sister's wedding, and the atmosphere was buzzing with enthusiasm. The Haldi ceremony was in full swing, with vibrant colors, laughter, and music filling the air. Friends and family had gathered to celebrate this special occasion.

Paloma looked stunning in her attire—a beautiful Rajasthani lehenga adorned with intricate embroidery. She had her hair styled in an elegant messy bun, adding to her charm. Her happiness radiated from her face, and it was evident to everyone present that she was truly enjoying every moment of this festive day.

Amidst the festivities, while helping Somali with various wedding tasks, paloma and Neel's phones chimed in unison. Curiosity got the better of her, and she couldn't resist checking it. As she read the email, her eyes widened with excitement. It was the news she had been eagerly waiting for—she had been selected for the job she had interviewed for, and so had Neel.

In the middle of all the cheerful noise and laughter, Paloma was unaware she was getting some eyes on her. The smile, her confidence was radiating through the atmosphere and someone couldn't look away. Someone she did not notice...

She immediately called Satya who was in Delhi, to share the thrilling news of her new job. Satya's voice shifted from warmth to unease as he processed the information that Paloma would have to relocate to Hyderabad for her new job. His initial reaction was not one of joy or congratulations; instead, it was a mixture of anxiety and frustration. Paloma moving to a different city meant a significant change in their relationship dynamics.

In their current situation, with Paloma living under her parents' roof, Satya had a certain level of control over her life. He could influence her decisions, and there was a sense of security in knowing she was nearby. However, with the job in Hyderabad, this control would slip away. She would be independent and self-reliant, and that prospect didn't sit well with Satya.

She ended the call abruptly, her heart pounding like a drum in her chest. In that moment, she realized she couldn't continue like this. The decision she was about to make weighed heavily on her, like a massive burden she could no longer carry. As she handed her phone to a classmate. Each step she took away from the ringing phone felt like a step towards freedom. She was embarking on a journey toward a future where she could finally breathe, where she could be her true self without fear or constraints.

In Somali's house, the evening sun painted the room with a warm, golden hue. Paloma stood in quiet solitude, surrounded by a gentle, almost ethereal light. Her lehenga lay gracefully on the bed, waiting to adorn her. Meanwhile, in the adjacent room, the atmosphere was entirely different. Laughter and banter filled the air as the boys of the gang readied themselves. Despite the physical separation, their shared energy and excitement for the evening transcended the walls that divided them.

Paloma stood in front of the mirror, her heart raced, not just from the excitement of the wedding, but from the realization that she couldn't tie the strings on her backless blouse.

After relentlessly trying the impossible for five minutes, "I need help!" she screamed, hoping that someone from the gang would come to her aid. Time ticked on, and her hope began to wane, until a knock on the door interrupted her pessimistic thoughts.

"Neel! Thank God," Paloma almost gasped, catching sight of him at the doorway. The room seemed to shrink, narrowing the focus down to the magnetic pull between them.

"You needed help..." Neel's voice trailed off, both locked in an intense gaze. In that moment, Paloma felt a desire so strong it threatened to consume her.

She bit her lip, her heart pounding, desperately yearning to kiss him. But instead, she turned away and presented her bare back to Neel. "I can't tie these," she murmured, her voice barely above a whisper.

Neel's breath hitched as he delicately grasped the laces of her blouse. Slowly, he pulled her closer, his touch electrifying her skin. Paloma held her breath, feeling every inch of her body craving him.

As he skillfully tied the laces, the tension between them grew unbearable. Finally, he turned Paloma around, their gazes locking once more. Without a word, their lips crashed together in a passionate embrace, igniting a fire that consumed them both.

They got rudely interrupted by Ruhan, barging in like a clumsy bull at a China shop.

"Are you guys' down... I am sorry... I meant... you know what? I will meet you downstairs" he left the room.

A sudden sense of guilt crept in with the door Ruhan opened. They didn't say anything to each other. Neel left saying "I... I will see if they need anything" Paloma nodded.

She grabbed herself back together and looked at the mirror saying, "Nothing happened" and left the room, with a curve faked in her face.

Downstairs, she spotted Ruhan, desperately attempting to ignore her. Determined not to let anyone kill her buzz, she pulled him aside, a mischievous glint in her eyes. "Hey Ruhan, I need a drink. Come!" she whispered, tugging him towards the bar.

"I didn't see anything," Ruhan tersely whispered as he poured whiskey into a plastic cup. Paloma drenched the alcohol, feeling it ignite a fire of courage within her. "Because nothing happened," she replied, her voice barely a whisper. "But you know what happened?"

"No, I definitely don't want to know," Ruhan protested vehemently.

Paloma grinned mischievously. "I broke up..." she began, relishing the reaction she was about to elicit. "How can you break up if there is nothing to break up?" Ruhan asked, confusion etched on his face. His eyes widened in realization. "Oh my god, you broke up with Satya!"

Paloma hushed him, heart pounding in her chest. "Shhh, not broke up broke up... but I disconnected his phone. I don't know where my phone is... but I made up my mind."

Ruhan stared at her, a mix of shock and admiration on his face. "You did what?" he exclaimed. Paloma smirked, finding a newfound sense of liberation. "I disconnected his phone, Ruhan. And it's about damn time."

The revelation hung in the air, the consequences of her actions yet to be fully realized. The wedding festivities continued around them, but Paloma's world had changed irreversibly, setting the stage for a new chapter in her life.

Chapter 13

THE SUNSET OF DECEMBER!

'Sham'. 'Amit Trivedi'. Sky painted in soft pastels. Air turns crisp. Breeze carrying a faint saint of winter. A handsome tall guy sitting beside her. Her face Lits up every time she drags from the joint. He is watching the sunset in her eyes.

You know the best part about making memories, you don't realize you're doing it.

Thc guy beside her, Arjya, is the stranger from the wedding. Turns out she was Somali's other group of friends.

They saw a boy, sixteen or seventeen, climbing into the gallery of the football ground where they were, sitting dangerously close to the gallery's edge. He seemed extremely upset, his voice filled with inaudible whispers as he stared down into the deep space below.

Without any hesitation, Arjya rushed to the boy, and pulled him away from the edge. It almost felt like he was about to jump. Paloma yelled at this young fellow, because she could see his face now. He was known for pulling these stunts for attention.

They looked at each other after the boy left. They burst out in laughter. She hasn't felt this light in lifetime.

"Wow, what a first date!" Arjya exclaimed, his eyebrows raised in amusement.

Paloma's smirk danced on her lips as she retorted, "Oh, so this is a date?"

The mention of labels made Arjya flinch slightly, but he quickly recovered, his voice tinged with uncertainty. "I mean, whatever you wanna call it..."

Paloma chuckled, a wry sense of humor lacing her words. "Let's not label this. Labels have never worked well for me anyway."

Her mind wandered, caught between the lingering presence of Satya, her ex-boyfriend, and the intoxicating memory of Neel's kiss. Satya and she had parted ways with unanswered questions, leaving her heart empty. And Neel, your heart doesn't just move on from a kiss like that overnight.

Yet fate had intervened in the form of an unknown profile messaging her on Instagram, a mere distraction from the chaos within her mind. A friend of Somali, Arjya. Somali told her that Arjya has confessed about the secret crush generated by her mesmerizing smile. Her heart wanted more when he texted that morning.

With every late-night call from Satya, Paloma would turn to Arjya, her newfound interest, just to keep her phone busy and her mind occupied. It was a delicate dance and an unfair one.

She thought it's always better not to label this one, because deep inside she knew, this was just a distraction to take her mind off Neel and Satya.

As Paloma stared into the distance, Arjya's voice broke through her thoughts, pulling her back to the present. "Beautiful, isn't it?"

Paloma turned to face Arjya, her lips curling into a mischievous smile. "It is... you know what?" she teased, her eyes twinkling with anticipation. "Are you afraid of heights?"

Arjya's eyes widened for a moment before he dramatically grabbed Paloma's hand, his expression playing out mock fear. "Don't tell me you're planning on jumping off this cliff. I can only be the hero once a day, you know," he quipped, a playful glint in his eyes.

Paloma laughed, her laughter ringing through the air like music. She pointed towards a colorful carnival in the distance. "Come," she said, her tone filled with an air of mystery.

She held Arjya's hand and guided him to a bustling carnival nearby. Picture this: warm, glowing lights hanging in the air, the delightful smell of cheap street food all around, and those thrilling yet slightly risky rides you often find at Indian carnivals. Amid the chaos of people talking, laughing, and the occasional scream from the wild rides, similar to what was going on inside her head.

They treated themselves to sweet cotton candy, munched on popcorn, and enjoyed watching some oddly entertaining talent shows. They tried their luck at shooting games and happily devoured pani puri until they couldn't eat another bite. Eventually, they ended up in front of a giant Ferris wheel.

"Care to join me on this whirlwind ride?" she teased, her voice playful.

Arjya, captivated by her infectious enthusiasm, couldn't resist. "Of course," he replied with a grin.

They ascended higher and higher, the world around them a blur of lights and laughter. Paloma's eyes sparkled with thrill as she looked at Arjya, he leaned in, and their lips brushed against each other I am momentary kiss. He tasted like a reckless life she never had, the perfect distraction. Paloma's cheeks flushed with a rosy hue, and Arjya heart raced even faster than before.

Little did she know Arjya was getting swept away by the intoxicating whirlwind of their budding romance, amidst the carnival's enchanting chaos...

As Paloma and Arjya strolled back towards home, her phone chimed with a text message. The screen displayed a message from none other than little prince charming.

"Can we talk?" he asked.

Paloma felt a rush of mixed emotions. Maybe, she thought, this was the moment she'd get the answers to all her lingering questions. She replied cautiously, "Sure, do you want to meet?"

"Where are you?" came his swift response.

"I'm near the college campus," she typed out.

"Okay... be there in fifteen minutes," he messaged back, replied

"Everything's all right?" Arjya inquired; his concern evident.

Paloma nodded, giving a half-hearted smile. "Yeah... yeah. I'll be meeting a friend after this..."

Arjya seemed hesitant but determined to express himself. "Hey Paloma, listen, it was lovely... meeting you. We should..."

But Paloma interrupted him mid-sentence, her tone tinged with a hint of melancholy. "Don't fall for me, Arjya…" She paused for a moment before continuing, her voice softer. "I had fun as well, but let's keep it that way... I am not the one..."

Arjya gazed into Paloma's eyes, struggling to find a response to her words. As the bus arrived, he simply said, "That's me... see you?"

"You will," Paloma replied with a faint smile.

Paloma and Neel found a quiet bench on the campus, away from the hustle and bustle. If you look at them from afar, they were not looking like lovers. Two friends, who would talk about anything in their life.

Neel told paloma why he looked visibly upset. Instead of his charming self, Nazia managed to cheat on him, with her ex, Pritam. It took Paloma no time to identify this name. She has heard this name from Neel more than she should, but the name is more important because this guy Pritam is a friend of Paloma's new friend,. whose lips still taste like hers.

But it was not a time to think about that. Neel was clearly heartbroken. We all clearly saw it coming except him. And what about the kiss? Which one? The one we waited so long, and wrote books about? Was it just a mistake for him?

As they sat there in that lonely bench, they had questions. About themselves, about each other. About what's going to happen next

Chapter 14

STARRY STARRY NIGHT…

"Drops of Jupiter" by "the train" the car stopped at a lonely road. A girl hurried to use the toilet nearby.

"Paloma?" called a familiar voice. The door opened with a cluck. Sleepy eyes and vertigo has taken most of her.

"Come here," he said. "Look up"

A distant murmur of the song floats in the air, to make this moment more memorable…

"*And tell me, did you fall for a shooting star?*

One without a permanent scar…"

When she looked up she saw a clear sky, full of stars. A distant mountain overlapping another, and a mild sound of some beetles.

It's cold, her cheeks were numb until he placed a peck on them. She enjoyed his warmth. He caressed her cheeks looking at her eyes.

"Come let's go, I'm done," said the girl using the toilet, breaking the spell of nature. They hopped in the car and faded in the alleys of the mountain road. A gush of cold wind hit her like a flashback.

Paloma and Arjya had been spending a lot of time together, bonding over shared music and rooftop joints at their college. They quickly became close friends, relishing each other's company. One evening, as they sat alone on the bleachers, Arjya surprised Paloma with an invitation: "I'm heading to Darjeeling, Paloma. Come with me."

Paloma chuckled, treating it like a jest. "Come with me," she echoed mockingly. "What if you turn out to be a serial killer? I barely know you."

Arjya, with a hint of earnestness, explained, "Our friend Sayan had to cancel due to exams. I'm serious about this, Paloma."

Paloma remained silent, staring into the distance. There was something genuine about him that drew her in.

As Arjya waited for Paloma's response, the cool breeze played with their hair, and the distant sounds of the city added a background melody to the moment. Paloma couldn't help but smile at Arjya's earnestness.

Breaking the brief silence, Arjya spoke again, his tone soft yet sincere, "I promise I'm not a serial killer, Paloma. I just want to spend time with you, get to know you better, and have some fun in Darjeeling. It'll be an adventure. Tell me atleast you will think about it? you don't have to answer now"

"Fine, I will think about it" Paloma replied, not able to refuse him.

But that day at the christmas party, when Paloma invited Arjya to Ruhan's place... after spending quite some time playing games and laughing, Paloma went to the balcony away from Pratim and away from the chaos. Arjya's friend (Nazia's ex) dancing like a stripper on the table. Neel and Samarth were not there in the Party. Neel had escaped to the mountains to deal with life. It's been a lot of things happening with Nazia, and the kiss with Paloma. He has to figure out what he likes, what he wants to do.

Breaking Paloma's solace, Arjya interjected, "I know Pratim can be a little..."

"Fun?" Paloma finished his sentence with a playful smile. "Don't worry about it."

"Come here," Arjya gently pulled Paloma by her waist. "You are freezing." He placed his warm hands on her numb ones, to comfort against the chilly night.

"I like you, snowball. I feel at home with you," Arjya confessed in a shy tone, his words carrying a sincerity that warmed the cold air between them.

"Darjeeling… you guys are leaving tomorrow?" Paloma asked, a part of her wanted to spend more time with him, to know him. But the other part was chaotic, hungered for self sabotage to feed the devils.

The prospect of being away from Paloma for five days now felt like a considerable stretch. He cherished her company and the thought of being apart for an extended period was beginning to weigh on him. Arjya took a deep breath, contemplating how to express his feelings.

"I was really looking forward to the trip, Paloma," he confessed, his eyes finding hers again. "But now, I can't help but think about being away from you for so long."

She showed Arjya a confirm ticket and said "too bad, i was looking forward to meeting you in Darjeeling"

And he couldn't believe it. He checked the tickets by zooming in at its max level, and when his frontal lobe confirmed, His amygdala couldn't resist saying "I love you Paloma!"

Was it just the excitement or he meant it? You never know.

Why did she go to Darjeeling? Maybe she enjoyed Arjya's company, Maybe the idea of being alone in the festive season sank her heart. Maybe she finally got out of a relationship with Satya and finally can do whatever she wants to do.

A quaint dormitory, nestled in a less-traveled village near Nepal, welcomed them with its rustic charm. The sudden drop in temperature hit Arjya and Paloma like a wave, causing them to shiver

Paloma wrapped her arms around herself, attempting to shield from the biting cold. "I didn't expect it to be this cold," she remarked, her breath visible in the frosty air.

Arjya, his breath forming small clouds, chuckled and pulled Paloma closer. "Well, we are in the mountains, snowball. Come here" he wrapped his arms around her. His friends laughed with joy seeing Arjya like this. They are seeing him happy after a long time. And he was not shy to show his affection.

They all settled in quickly underneath the warmth of their blankets, the intimacy of the group adding to the coziness of the mountain dormitory. As the night deepened, and the room grew dim, Paloma found herself unable to shake off the chill, her feet growing cold. Feeling her discomfort, Arjya tightened his embrace, pulling her a little too close to himself. The subtle warmth of their shared body heat, smelled of wine and fireplace.

"You didn't reply," Arjya whispered beneath the blanket, his words carrying a vulnerability that echoed.

She knows exactly what he is talking about. Does she know what to answer? Is she the right person for him? Isn't she too complicated to be his?

In a soft murmur, she admitted, "I know we're on a ship, Arjya, sailing through the unknown. But I'm not sure yet which port it will turn to. Maybe we'll discover new shores together, or maybe our paths will lead us in different directions."

As the uncertainty lingered in the air, Arjya's heart couldn't bear to waste another moment without her. In a burst of emotion, he pressed his lips against hers with an intensity that conveyed all the unspoken feelings within him. The kiss felt like a decadent cheesecake melting in your mouth – a blend of sweetness and warmth. She moaned softly and he pressed his lips deeper. The layers of woolen clothes that had shielded them from the cold now became a barrier, and their bodies yearned for the touch of bare skin.

they held their breaths, the rhythmic melody of their heartbeats, speaking volumes in a language that transcended words.

"I don't care about the port, Arjya. I love sailing with you," she whispered,

Did his eyes lit up a bit hearing this? Was she leading him on for no reason? Was she actually enjoying his company? Then why did she keep reminding herself she is not the one for him.

He dozed off in her arms, and she couldn't help·but watch him with a smile. His innocence was contagious, and she recollected his silly words. Gently, she caressed his face, careful not to disturb his peaceful sleep,

The next morning, she woke up naked underneath the blanket and his face still held the calmness to shatter her chaos. It was freezing cold yet she decided to open the window, outside it she could clearly see the kanchenjunga range... She gently woke him up. He settled into the crook of her neck as they witnessed the sun casting a warm, orange hue upon the pristine white mountain range. The beauty of the sunrise against the majestic backdrop.

"I see an amazing skyline when you are around," she whispered, her fingers gently playing with his hair. He felt like peace.

As they took that extra mile to reach the hill's summit, a serene landscape unfolded before them. It felt like peace as he stood by her side, absorbing the breathtaking view, and softly declared, "It cannot be more perfect." A kiss sealed the sentiment.

It felt like peace when they found a secluded bench near the slope of Darjeeling's mountains. The melody of "December er Shohor" played softly, harmonizing with the hues of the setting sun. It was a moment suspended in time.

They walked hand in hand along the Mall Road in Darjeeling. The town was buzzing with life, and the air carried the scent of freshly made tea from nearby shops. The Himalayan mountains stood tall in the distance, it was very difficult for Paloma not to fall for him. It all seemed so perfect. She felt seen in his eyes, she felt heard when he was around...

It would be a perfect love story if they decided to stay in Darjeeling. It would be like a surprising twist in a movie, if they left everything and made a life there. Maybe he could open a nice little shop on Mall Road, selling cool stuff. And she could set up a stall selling tasty Maggi and momos, making the air smell amazing.

But reality was far from the picturesque dreams. The day arrived when they sat on the train to head back home. Arjya's eyes were soft, and he spoke with a trembling voice, "I will miss waking up beside you." His words cracked, and he turned to look out of the window, attempting to hide the tears that welled up. she couldn't hold herself back. "I think I love you too," she said, wrapping her arms around him from behind..

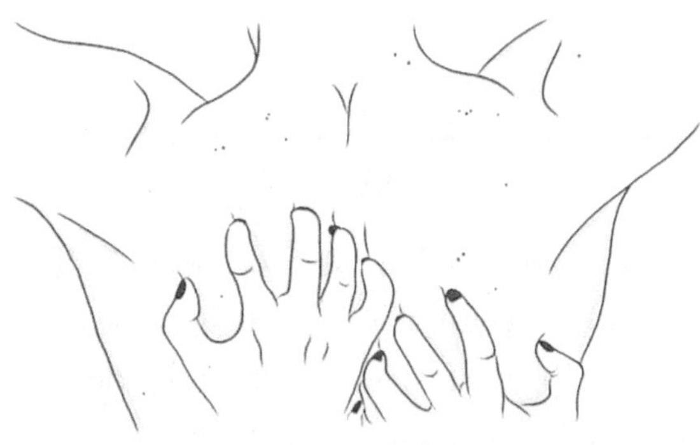

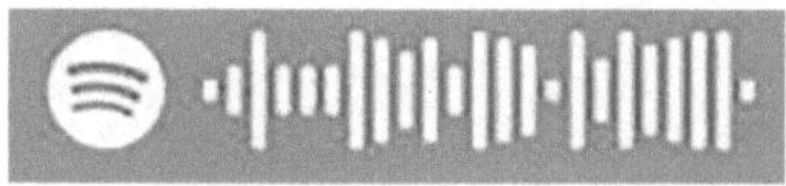

Chapter 15

A SIMPLE MOVIE DATE?

"What did you delete" Paloma replied to Neels deleted messages in the morning.

"Nothing, I just wished you good night and thought you don't deserve it" Neel replied after almost two hours.

Neel has been acting strange after the trip. For him the trip he went to was for self-introspection. Especially what happened in Somali's sister's wedding. Especially about Paloma. For Paloma it was the exact opposite. She went to the trip so that she didn't have to think.

Their last conversation before the trip was something like this,

Paloma, sitting next to Neel in an empty classroom, declared, "Single life, lit life."

Neel responded with a touch of sarcasm, "Everything new has its own charms, until it fades away." He knew Paloma well; she wasn't one to remain single for long, as she thrived on being around people.

Playfully, Paloma swatted Neel, saying, "Don't try to scare me."

Neel carefully avoided her playful hit, replying, "I'm just saying."

Defeated but undeterred, Paloma unlocked her phone to show him something. "See this," she said, displaying a photo of him shirtless in Goa. The picture had been secretly taken by Paloma and edited. Neel was no stranger to this; most of his Instagram photos were secretly captured by her.

Neel quipped, "Your personal production, I'm sure."

Paloma, attempting sarcasm, retorted, "Who else has so much free time to invest in you."

"I am not laughing" Neel said.

"You know what? I didn't even like you that much" Paloma said playfully.

"Sure, I believe you" Neel replied with confidence.

Neel's return from the trip had ignited a spark of hope within him. He believed that perhaps this was the right moment to take his relationship with Paloma to the next level, a step he had hesitated to take for a long time. He could sense a change in the air, a shift in the dynamics between them, and it filled him with optimism.

Eager to convey his newfound willingness to give them a chance, Neel headed back to the network zone, hoping to share his thoughts with Paloma, but he was met with a series of unexpected posts. Paloma had shared romantic pictures and stories with Arjya, that is not very casual. Taylor Swift's "Lover." Playing behind those pictures and stories.

The sight of these posts left Neel in a state of bewilderment and heartache. The hope he had built up was suddenly challenged by a surge of uncertainty and confusion. It was evident that Paloma had moved on with someone else, and Neel found himself standing at a crossroads, unsure of which path to take next.

"It's raining again.

That feeling, again.

Never forgotten.

I wanted every rain,

Every monsoon

Every winter

Every summer

All of them with you.

Naive? Maybe.

But I liked this childish me.

Every drop of rain felt like you!

That could never be mine.

You know why mountains are my favorite?

Because they are so beautiful, that I can only gaze and admire them.

But I can never touch it, Just like you.

I wish I could climb those fears of yours.

But it's not mine to conquer anymore.

Maybe I'm that traveler, who can never go beyond.

Ohh!! I so wish to explore the possibilities beyond reach.

But my trip has ended.

Time to come back home.

Back to reality.

Only regret., I couldn't bring you back with me.

But you belong there.

I know.

You will always be that journey that I can never forget.

Those memories I made.

I'll cherish them till my last breath.

I Hope you find your traveler

Your conqueror."

This was the message Neel deleted that night, and it was more than a goodnight message. But we are talking about Neel, the man who wears heartbreaks as his armour, shits brick Inside but makes the shell so thick that you can't see tears. He was like superman in love with kryptonite, all of them, he didn't know how strong they were till it hurt him.

The equation between Arjya and Paloma changed and not for good. Paloma did not deal with her breakup or the feeling she had for Neel. Poor Arjya unaware of all these became the usual self he always were. Time went by, and Arjya kept thinking everything was all right. But the truth was, there were bugs inside the perfect looking apple.

It would be so great if we could create a device like X-ray, to peep through someone's soul. A neon light under which you can see the bold naked feelings. Things would have been so easier for everyone.

What kept Paloma going was the deep conversations about life's goals, deep unattended feelings, and a sweet healthy friendship with Neel. As Arjya was hardly present, and never alone, the late night chats with the best friend became a ritual.

Crazy sex weekly twice and party weekly thrice was what left of Paloma and Arjya after three months from the trip. With no privacy from his friends, they missed the riming pattern of their relationship. And the biggest problem was, he was not a bad guy. Paloma liked his innocence, his silly jokes, the power play that she had with him... but deep down she always knew he was not the guy.

Paloma wanted to do the good thing, to be in a monotonous relationship, not to hurt Arjya but in the process, she forgot it was not the right thing. She never loved Arjya maybe she adored him, she cared for him, she liked him, but it was no love, and she knew that.

It was a cold winter evening, when most of the students went home from the college football ground. Ruhan was on his way to the campus, after meeting his girlfriend, so Neel and Paloma decided to wait for Ruhan.

The campus was dominated by a large building. In front of this ediface, lay a football ground, complete with galleries. Further behind the building, tucked away, was the generator area along with a smaller field... It became an unofficial hangout spot for those looking for a quieter place to chat, contemplate, or share a smoke. Here, amidst the hum of generators and the soft glow of artificial light, where conversations and bonds were forged. It was a place where ideas and stories were exchanged, where friendships deepened, and where solitude held its own charm in the midst of university life.

Neel sat upon the concrete structure and Paloma stood in front of him.

"Oh bhai, I told you no? I went to this wedding yesterday" Neel said with a spark in his eyes...

"Yes, the one where you enjoyed a few too many drinks with your relatives; how could I ever forget?" Paloma responded.

"There was this girl, quite young, around eleventh grade, I suppose," Neel mentioned.

"Quite the Casanova, aren't you?" Paloma playfully teased.

"Arreh, I was not even sure she was my relative or not, it was some risky flirting I did" Neel confessed.

Paloma had shifted her position and was now leaning on Neel, standing between his legs.

“Did you get laid?” Paloma asked casually

“Regrettably, no, my dear friend. My wedding make-out checklist has been updated,” Neel said in a flirtatious tone.

“Who? When?” Paloma asked, a hint of surprise in her voice, while she gazed at Neel, who gave her a subtle nod.

“Are we counting me?” Paloma blushed a little.

“Should we not?” Neel pressed a little more.

“Wow, I am on one of your checklists...” Paloma said this with a sense of accomplishment.

“What would I do without you?” Neel said playfully.

“Want to catch the new movie, Dwitio Purush?” Paloma suggested, her eyes sparkling with excitement.

Neel nodded, a hint of eagerness in his voice. “I’ve heard it’s getting fantastic reviews.”

Paloma’s lips curled into a smile. “How about tomorrow at 8 pm? You, me, and Ruhan?”

Neel, sitting behind her, gently wrapped his arms around her, and she rested her head against his chest. “8 pm, huh? Sounds great. Why not stay at my place afterward? That way, we can avoid the late-night hassle.”

In that moment, akin to the pulsing generator lights, their hearts raced to a common beat, a silent understanding passing between them, hinting at the possibilities that a night together might bring.

When the murmurs of the other room stopped, they knew their dear friend Ruhan had gone to sleep. They were waiting for the moment, the white noises in the dark screaming louder than ever. He looked like a sculpture made by someone who had magic in their hands, work of art. The dimly lit room, by the warm street light.

With one look at each other, they both knew the desires been piling up way too long. Neel's look piercing through her flesh, Paloma was wearing a peach toned satin slip dress and a sheer lace kimono on top of that. She traced the outline of her lower lips with her thumb and gently worked her way down to the knot of the belt tying the kimono together. With a firm and quick pull, she untied the knot and the kimono fell apart on the ground.

He could see her perfectly done imperfect hairdo, The soft golden tint upon the swells of her breasts vanishes in the perfect contour of her cleavage. She tilts her head exposing her neck, and in an inviting manner slips the right strap of her dress. He realized in no time it was gonna be a show. He played 'I put a spell on you' by 'Annie Lennox'

Paloma fierce, dragged a chair nearby, she sat backwards in the chair, facing him, her legs spreading wide, her dress climbs up her thighs, exposing her carefully chosen lace panties. Maintaining the eye contact she opens up her bun, and with a shift motion, lets her hair fall upon her almost bare back. She bends forward and her fingers traced her thighs climbed higher and she grabs the end of her slip dress, she started pulling her dress up exposing her black lingerie. She lifts up both her arms, teasing him enough. She remembers how he says, "not showing is sexier than showing" while her one hand traced the other hand until it reached her back, while her other hand hung high in air. She dropped the satin on the floor and got up on her toes. The lace lingerie on her warm skin tone felt magical.

She came forward towards Neel who was sitting and enjoying the show at the corner of his bed, with a grin on his face. She climbed the bed and sat on his lap with both legs spread wide open. She could feel what she had done to him. He smelled woody and musky like usual. The only smell she craved for in every man, every night, every hotel room. His hand crawls up her back. Her lips touching his earlobes, her breath sending shivers down his spine.

He let her play with him quite a long time, he loves this version of her, the confident version. His patience wore thin, he grabbed her face with both hands and before kissing her he smiled looking at her eyes. He bit her lower lips first,

"That's for teasing me with it" he said

She moaned softly, her hands reached for the button of his shirt, while lips danced upon his. Once done Neel took his shirt off, and his chiseled muscles flexed themselves. Paloma's hands were tracing lines from his back, with a sudden surprise he lifted her up standing near the bed and threw her on the soft mattress. He worked his way up between her legs and removed her panties. He placed few kisses on both her inner thighs. Her body arched grabbing his hair, and he looked at her with pride.

"You know what's a man's strongest muscle?" Neel asked. Paloma looked at him with needy eyes. She bit her lips and said "What?"

"Let me show you" he said diving deep in between her legs. The room echoed with sounds of her moans, she never experienced something so divine before. Unlike other men in her bed, he feels pleasure when a woman moans with desire, he takes pride in giving them what they desire. He knows patience and claiming what's his. He knows where to stop to keep the fun going.

He takes out the belt around his waist and ties her hands to the bedpost.

"Is this what you want?" Neel asked

"Um hmm" she replied, her voice barely a breath.

"Tell me what you want me to do next" he probed more

This is completely new thing for her, she is used to giving up in bed. She is used to powerlessness. But he likes to push her out of the comfort zone. He wants her to beg for what she wants.

"I want you to...tear my bra"

A devilish smirk played upon Neel's lips as he slowly reached for the clasp. The sound of tearing fabric filled the room as the last remnants of restraint crumbled away. Paloma's heart raced in her chest.

"I want you to touch me" she said in a trembling voice.

"Touch you where?" He came so close to her breasts that his lips almost touched her, but it didn't. "Here?" he asked his breath made her shiver.

"Yes, please" she pleaded,

He kissed everywhere, but where her body needed him to. She tried with every ounce of her strength to push her body.

"I know what you want Paloma, you only gonna get if you ask" Neel instructed.

"I need you to kiss my nipples" she begged.

Well, that's all he needed. His tongue danced upon her perked nipples, and she moaned his name louder. He put two of his fingers in her mouth and she licked it like a good girl. He wants her to lose control now...

his hand sliding between her thighs, finding the wetness that awaited him. She lifts her body up with utmost pleasure. His lips on her left nipple while inserting his fingers inside her.

"Not so soon. I am just getting started" Neel instructed when Paloma was about to let go.

Neel unzipped himself and rubbed himself to tease her a little more. He untied her hand, and she clasped his perfectly built back. He understood she would not be able to resist much longer. He swiftly pushed himself inside her.

The Rythm becomes madning with the increasing pace. Her legs trembled, and the room filled with heavy breath, he pulled himself out.

He got up from the bed, a little restless, about to finish when Paloma said, "let me..."

Paloma knelt down in front him and her lips hovered over Neel's dick, and with a mischievous smile, she took him into her mouth. His groans of pleasure filled the room, driving her to increase her pace, relishing his intoxicating taste. He grabbed her hair in a pony to have a good grip on her. Occasionally he would push a little harder in her mouth to hear her gag.

They sat by the window naked, sharing a smoke after the perfect sex of her life. The room is so silent you can hear the tobacco burning. She leans on his shoulders. It felt perfect.

But one day at a time...

Chapter 16

THE COURTROOM OF SOCIAL MEDIA

"Hey, there's no way to say goodbye" by Leonard Cohen played softly. Trembling hands held onto the memories. Ashes of cigarettes scattered like fragments of the past. The soothing sound of the river flowed, the roads comparatively empty, setting the stage for world's greatest pandemic.

Everytime the boat stopped in the nearby jetty, eyes eagerly scanned the surroundings, hopeful to see a familiar face. Perhaps a known figure would emerge, questioning with eyes that silently asked, "Why did you do this to me?" And maybe, just maybe, she would summon the courage to say, "Will you forgive me?" In that moment, they might lock eyes, and perhaps, in that gaze, they would find a way to let go of the tangled threads that bound them.

But that boat never came to the river bank; she waited for him. But Arjya Never came. She waited, like she said she would, and he did not come like he said he wouldn't...

"On the other side of the river, maybe you're there,
A pocket watch ticking, a love left in the air.
I'm lost in an audio drama, swallowing guilt inside,
Without my glasses, a blurry world, nowhere to hide.

It felt like you came to meet me, but it wasn't you,
A fleeting hope in the blur, a sad déjà vu.
No one feels quite like you, it's true,
Did our hearts skip a beat? I wonder, do you?
The kiss on the hill-top hard to forget,
A twisted cry inside, full of regret.

The city across the river isn't mine anymore,

No one's here to sing a lullaby, like before.

In the quiet street, my heart fades away,

Alone, in echoes, our stories replay."She wrote with her red pen in a diary. Each line felt like her heart's bleeding, the ink capturing the weight of her emotions on the paper.

But what was she expecting? Did she believe her secrets would remain unspoken? Did she think she could escape without consequence?

Sometimes the madness in our head is difficult to explain in words. Sometimes we act on our impulses and create an illusion. Of a world? a person? a situation? But reality has its own ways of challenging our delusions.

Neel and Paloma decided they didn't want to be in a relationship. Why? Well, Paloma was already in one, and Neel wasn't ready to commit. Did they talk about it clearly? Obviously not. Instead, Neel texted, "Close your eyes, and listen to this: *'Snuff' by Corey Taylor.*"

"I only wish you weren't my friend

Then I could hurt you in the end

I never claimed to be a saint

Ooh, my own was banished long ago

It took the death of hope to let you go" Paloma quoted the line of the song after listening to it.

"So, if you love me let me go

And run away before I know

My heart is just too dark to care

I can't destroy what isn't there" Neel quoted back

"If you still care don't ever let me, go" she quoted the line but it felt like a plea

"Tell me all these Paloma when you are single" a hint of hurt typed itself out.

In the days that followed, Paloma and Neel made a conscious effort to be the best versions of themselves. They decided to redefine their relationship, steering away from the complexities of romance and choosing to be the friends they both deserved.

That day when Nazia called him, he was taking the last drag of his smoke in his usual spot.

"Are you awake? Are you busy? Can we talk?" she said

"Usual spot. Usual things" he replied.

After all these while if there was one person who can change Neel's commitment phobia, it was her. The fighter in him, tired and battered,takes a backseat. Flight seemed the only option this time. Neel was not afraid of love; He flew inside the darkness for the light he had always craved.

Did she have the light or the warmth? Only he knows…

"Tomorrow is Sunday, I know you don't have work, meet me face to face" she said

"I will call you if I can," he said. He tried not to care, but he did.

He knew exactly what he wanted. He craved the familiarity of her scent, the warmth of her smile playing at the corners of her lips. He longed for the playfulness in her tantrums, the depth in her eyes, and the comforting touch of her hands in his hair.

It's always tough to forget the first person you allowed yourself to be vulnerable with.

"On my way" he said to Nazia when Sunday evening came.

As they lit up a cigarette, the first puff created a cloud, one that seemed no darker than the one already hanging over his head.

Seeing Neel move on pretty quickly made her shatter from inside. Questions appeared in the form of insecurity. She never realized it's not only Neel who did not take the leap for her, she always made him feel like the other guy. No matter how much you care for someone, love someone, if you are not ready to fight for them someone else will. When she expected someone to fight for her, she should have it in her to fight for them as well.

Despite Arjya's efforts to include Paloma in everything, attempting to make her feel at home, she couldn't fully reciprocate. Perhaps the guilt of betraying the one person she should have treated right weighed heavily on her. Did she ever truly love that guy?

College was almost over, and classes were not a big deal anymore. Neel and Ruhan were interning at a company, while Samarth decided to pursue art after engineering. Somali was studying for a better job.

In the midst of their busy lives, there was something bigger happening. News channels were talking about a virus that could spread easily. If people didn't take precautions, it might become a global pandemic.

And in a day like this, when Narendra modi our prime minister finally addressed the complete lockdown saying no one will get out of their homes for next few days unless it's life or death situation, Paloma received a text from Neel,

"I need to tell Nazia about us" Neel texted struggling to find the right words

"About us?" Paloma reconfirmed.

Nazia, being Pratim's ex, was an integral part of Arjya's group. Paloma realized that once this information was out, it would spread like wildfire. A fire that had the potential to consume everything – her innocence, her connection with Arjya, and the only thread keeping her from falling apart.

“Are you sure?” she said with a gulp in her throat.

Could he really do this to her? With his good conscience? Nobody knew her better than he did. After all these years, was he asking for her conscience to be the executioner of her soul?

“I feel if I don’t tell her, and this relationship fails, I will subconsciously blame myself” Neel confessed “and if it works out, she will never know a part of me”

So, in the end, it’s all about morals, being the good guy? And what about her? Should she be fed to the crocodile? If someone had to wield that power, maybe it should be him.

She did not think about love or hate at that moment. She saw her friend needed to do something to be happy. It didn’t feel like a betrayal.

“Do it. I will take care of the storm” Paloma assured him.

“Are you sure?” Neel questioned. perhaps because he couldn’t believe this would be such an easy conversation with Paloma.

“If it were just my story, I might hesitate. But it’s our story, equally. I’m willing to share the burden, to carry it together,” Paloma expressed sincerely.

"Do you love Arjya?" Neel asked, on the verge of taking a drastic step.

"Regardless of love, he doesn't deserve all the hurt," Paloma replied with a weight of consideration in her words.

It felt like Arjya was taking the whip for something he didn't even do. She felt like running away. Away from all this chaos.

She was decently drunk when Nazia called her, and she knew she couldn't ignore her any longer.

"Was it all planned or happened in the heat of the moment?" Nazia asked, choosing her words carefully.

Paloma was about to answer, but something inside her sensed a nuance. A woman whose man slept with you wouldn't call and ask if it was planned unless she had something to prove. Maybe she would cry and blame and use curse words. But the calmness inside Nazia sent chills down her spine.

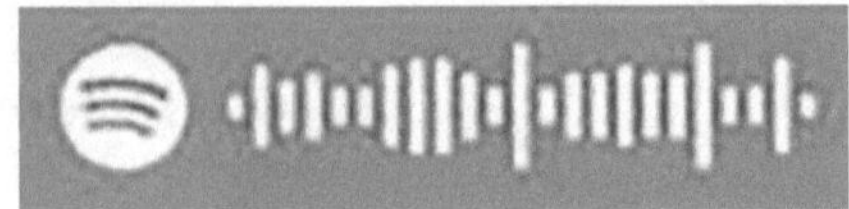

And at that moment, it became a game. A game of betrayal and innocence. This was the Paloma; Satya had created in those years. She remembered how the thin line between truth and lie depends on how you tell something, how effortlessly you can manipulate the situation and how easy it was to play with humans.

It was no longer about friendship, love, compassion. It was about protecting the innocence of her or of Arjya's.. The angel inside her takes a silent back seat, when the devil starts its dance.

Shortly after this, her phone buzzed. The name "Pratyush", Arjya's best friend, displayed on her phone screen felt like the declaration of war.

But pratyush said "we cant find Arjya Paloma!" with a terror in his voice.

This is what she was the most afraid about. She was ready for war but not like this. Not sacrificing the one person she cared about.

Unable to understand who to turn to, Paloma panicked. She tried calling Arjya repeatedly. He did not answer, and honestly why would he?

"Tell us the truth, Paloma. We will help you... tell us what happened that night," Pratim attempted to coax the real story out of her, thinking he could outsmart her. Little did he know, he was taking a page straight from her mother's playbook, she grew up with,

"Ask Nazia if he hasn't done this before..." Paloma had played her first trump card, revealing that Neel had previously misled Nazia about a kiss between him and Paloma to incite jealousy.

"What is she talking about, Nazia?" Shromona inquired, her voice tinged with concern.

Nazia's response carried a hint of defeat, "See, guys, Neel once told me he kissed Paloma when they didn't, to make me jealous. But this is different."

"How do you know it's different?" Pratim pressed, clearly influenced by the age-old sentiment where your ex's present is always seen as an enemy.

Pratyush suggested, "Let's bring Neel onto this call. We can figure this out together."

As the night progressed and Arjya remained missing, did Paloma feel a tinge of concern? Did she ever experience a hint of guilt? Were all her tears merely a façade? It was impossible to discern. She was a method actor in her life, blurring the lines between truth and deceit, leaving even herself uncertain of what was real.

"I am not picking up the call," Neel texted.

"Arjya is missing!" Paloma seeked moral support.

"It's all because of me. I am so sorry. Please forgive me" Neel cried his heart out.

There's no point in thinking about all these now. The deed's been done. But there is crack, that allows guilt to come in,

Away from all this, Arjya felt like his world had crashed in front of his eyes. It had only been three months since they had been seeing each other, but for him, it meant way more than it did for Paloma. He ran away to a place where he used to go for solace. He did not pick up anyone's calls or reply to anyone's messages. He never felt a betrayal like this before. He quietly sat in a place and replayed everything in her head more than 10 times, trying to find out what went wrong.

His heart held onto the cherished memories, like how Paloma patiently waited for him during his nerve-wracking first job interview. She adored him with a warmth that made him feel like a younger version of herself. Her care extended to the smallest details, and she took the time to look after him in ways that spoke volumes about her affection and concern. It was these moments of tenderness and consideration that lingered in his heart, making the current situation even more painful. He knew in his heart that she was lying, he knew everything about Neel and her before they started dating.

His friends felt his hurt and their anger boiled up more. They went to all the pictures of Neel and Paloma posted online, and commented things like "being best friends means getting into each other's pants"

The fight was worth winning with the love of her life, fighting alongside him. She expected a poetic justice, where they both lose a part of the battle as a lost ship, they would collide with each other like the wild waves, unaware that the waves crash on the rocks during moments of weakness, and the rocks gradually decay beneath the relentless force. And every time the wave goes back, it goes back to the ocean…

Who was her ocean? The only person that came to her mind was the Satya. But she chose to leave that, allowing it to sink into the depths of her darkness, unattended. In the vast sea of emotions, she abandoned the one source of solace, watching it submerge into the abyss of her own making.

There was only one guy, one of Arjya's friends who showed mercy to Paloma. He tried to calm the situation. Connect Paloma with Arjya to short the whole mess face to face.

"Meet me, just once," she pleaded the next day when that friend finally got Arjya on call.

"I won't, I can't," Arjya replied with moist eyes. Maybe he would have if she had told the truth.

"I will wait in our place" her voice desperate.

"I won't come Paloma" his voice laced with ununderstood hurt mixed anger.

When she left, she lost the shred of self respect along with her purse. She waited for him for five hours. He kept his promise. He did not come.

Paloma stared at her phone, contemplating whether to reply to Neel's text. The message simply asked, "Hey, how are you holding up?"

After a few minutes, she decided to be honest. "Not great. Arjya didn't show up."

Neel felt like a villain in Paloma's story. He felt selfish and he didn't quite like a feeling. When he was talking to Nazia late that night, he complained how Arjya stood Paloma up. Unknowingly Neel hammered the final nail in Paloma's coffin. Nazia confronted Arjya. He, unable to comprehend the situation, decided to shut Paloma out of his life completely, deleting her number and any trace of her existence from his phone.

"Don't spoil twenty nine nights just to be happy in one" was the last thing Paloma told Neel with a tone she never thought she would have for Neel. She misunderstood him, blocked him from everywhere. He lost everything that night. The love of his life and the best friend.

Was this the end of them? Maybe…

Chapter 17

PAROLE IS OVER

Paloma's reflection in the mirror betrayed the fatigue and pain she carried. One evening, she decided she couldn't bear the weight any longer.

At the salon, the hairdresser, sensing Paloma's silent anguish, asked, "What are we doing today?"

Paloma, with a mix of determination and vulnerability, uttered, "Chop it off. I need a fresh start." Her long, beautiful hair now felt like an anchor dragging her into the depths of heartache.

As the scissors snipped away the strands, each falling lock echoed the pain she'd endured. The hairdresser, empathetic to her unspoken story, said, "Sometimes, a change on the outside helps heal what's inside."

After that difficult night, when Paloma's life felt shaky, a big problem was on the way – the pandemic. It made everything harder. The streets, once busy, were now like ghost towns with no people around. Shops closed down, making the neighborhoods look empty. Paloma, dealing with her own problems, walked through these silent streets. She had no friends she could trust, and there was no one to turn to. In those days when Paloma felt alone, social media turned into a source of unkindness. People were being mean to her, calling her hurtful names. Each comment felt like a virtual attack, making her feel even more lonely and isolated.

Sitting by the cliff on the second-floor terrace, her heart racing, Paloma thought about ending everything. Her usual fear of heights that used to stop her seemed to have disappeared. Now, she wasn't afraid of anything.

Was she brave or a coward? Taking one's own life is not an easy decision. It goes against the primal instinct to survive. Imagine the pain she was going through to try and overcome that deep-seated urge to live.

While sitting there, she decided to text her ex-boyfriend, Satya. They hadn't talked in a long time. She hoped he could provide some comfort. *It was an easier option than taking your own life, it cannot get any worse* she though

Her inability to learn from her mistakes is commendable. She repeated the same manual as before. She did not come clean to Satya as well. I think she started believing her own facade a little too much.

Paloma shared her version of events with Satya, saying, "Neel used my name to make Nazia feel jealous, and all of Arjya's friends didn't believe me. Arjya didn't even talk to me to hear my story." The familiar pattern of half-truths and avoiding full disclosure continued...

There was no point in doing this, but deep down she thought if people knew she cheated on someone, anyone, people would look at her differently. The ingrained people-pleaser in her resisted this change, and she was aware that, above all, Satya would be inclined to believe her version because that's what he wanted to believe.

But Satya learnt from his past mistakes. He asked, "So you're telling me you were never physically involved with Neel?"

Now, the first rule of lying is to look at the whole situation like an onion. The first rule was to withhold peeling a layer until absolutely necessary. And when peeling a layer of falsehood, it had to be a mistake worse than the previous one but better than the next...

"I mean, after we broke up and before I got into a relationship with Arjya, we kissed once. That's it. We were both drunk," she lied, keeping a straight face.

"Did he tell Nazia about that?" Satya took a shot in the dark.

Paloma knew what he needed to hear. Paloma knew he had to Sabotage her friends to make her story believable.

"No he did not. Because he was in a relationship when it happened" Paloma created an alternative storyline.

Did the light in her eyes doomed when Neel chose the broken wings of Nazia more than her devotion? Did the warmth disappear when Arjya stood her up that day? Or was she this cold from the beginning?

"I always told you he is not your friend. But you chose them over me!" Satya said, falling right into Paloma's web of lies.

In Satya's mind, he believed that Paloma had learned her lesson. Bringing her back into his life would give him complete control, or so he thought. Little did he know that Paloma, despite appearing submissive, was holding an invisible bridle—a silent strategy for self-preservation.

Was Paloma consciously plotting a tit-for-tat retaliation? Did she meticulously plan her moves, or did she impulsively seek refuge in the windowless house to escape the storm outside?

In a time when people couldn't return to their own homes due to the pandemic, the shelter without ventilation didn't seem to stress her out much.

"Never cut your hair short again; you don't look good in that," Satya instructed.

Did his statement already carry an underlying sense of control?

Couldn't she take a year for herself? Focus on her insecurities? Understand how to be a better person? What was she scared of? Nights where she will have no one to talk to? Mornings where no one will wait for her 'good morning' message? Someone to show care when she is not herself? Can all these overpower you to be yourself? One day she will be tired of someone else's skin again, she will be tired of proving herself, she will be tired of social standards.

Parole was over. And it's been a month of her being the perfect girlfriend.

"five years back on this day you asked me" Will you be my girl I remember the first time our eyes met, I remember the first time we giggled together, I remember the first time we kissed, I remember the first time we held hands. I remember how we grew up together. I remember how you called me the mirror image of yours. I cannot imagine my future without you, not even a bit. Dear love. I know I messed up everything really badly. I know that I couldn't do justice to your love for me. But this time things are different. With this bit I wanna say we are official. So love, cheers to our journey of growing old together. I love you" she was about to send this message to Satya, when her phone chimed.

Amongst other unnecessary notifications and the time showing 3am in the night, there was a name. A name that she thought will never cross the path with her.

Neel.

"Ludo khelibi? (wanna play ludo?" the message stirred up all the hidden emotions within her.

A friend who betrayed her. A friend who she betrayed. A lover who cared less. A love she never gave enough label. A story that started with a story. Complications that seem to vanish in each other's eyes. Yet they decided never to look at those eyes again.

When she was in 8th grade, she observed a small plant outside her classroom window, clinging to life on a gutter pipe of a nearby apartment building. It had pink flowers. Love is like that plant. No matter how smelly or inhabitable the situation is, love gives you pink flowers in the stomach. It is not calculated. It cannot be plotted. It's not easy to unlove people.

Chapter 18

WHATEVER YOU SAY

Wake up, log in by 9.30, reach out to several Prospects, and try to close the deal. Log out at 9.30. Have dinner with her family. Duty calls. Drink 2 pegs to sleep. This was her routine.

When days were passing away, with Paloma trying to fit in a world Satya designed for her, she pleaded with her company to give her an early joining and submerged herself in work. But because of the epidemic, her dream of going away from home remained uncatered. The entire world was working from home, and so was she.

Neel and Paloma are socially 'colleagues' now. At least the world knows that. Neel is under the team of that unfriendly interviewer. He seemed a lot more friendly now. However, Paloma's manager was a real pain in the ass. Fits the typical definition of a boss you crib about in your cigarette breaks. He texts her sometimes on Whatsapp seeing her photos and updates, congratulating her on closing deals.

It became a little easier for Paloma after joining work. Neel also seemed to change a lot. As college ended she took Paloma a little more seriously. He Never spoke to Nazia after that day, and niether did Paloma with Arjya.

Paloma's frustration wore thin after some months when Satya started having problems- the same problems he had with her college friends with Shree.

"Shree is not a friend of yours. She manipulates you" said Satya.

"But she is my childhood friend, the oldest" Paloma tried but couldn't resist being defensive.

"You fought for your friends before, look what they did to you. I am here to tell you what's good and what's not" he said in an authoritative tone.

"Whatever you say" said Paloma, defeated.

Whatever you say... but for how long?

In the morning, Paloma acts like a sweet, obedient girl, you'd introduce to your parents. But when night comes, she becomes a different person—stronger, more expressive, and unafraid to speak her mind. During the day, she puts on a friendly face, but at night, she lets her true self shine.

During the daytime, Paloma presents a facade of bidding farewell to certain friends in a post, strategically excluding her closest ones to please Satya. However, when night falls, she reaches out to those omitted friends, drunk. In the morning, she posts an image of modesty through her choice of clothing, while at night, she sheds inhibitions, stripping herself in front of strangers.

The plants flourished, turning greener, and Kolkata experienced a bearable summer. After a decade, Delhi witnessed the clearest sky of the year, with pollution levels drastically reduced. The Kanchenjunga range became visible from New Jalpaiguri. However, all these changes occurred due to a pandemic that claimed millions of lives of people who nurtured science and technology to manipulate nature for its own convenience over the years. When nature comes out after being suppressed and oppressed for so long, it brings changes-good and bad, but destruction first.

What Is it like trying to make friends with a wild animal? Sometimes, wild berries can be poisonous. It's like a scorpion choosing a fat frog as its prey—nature has its own ways. And when nature comes out it overpowers everything.

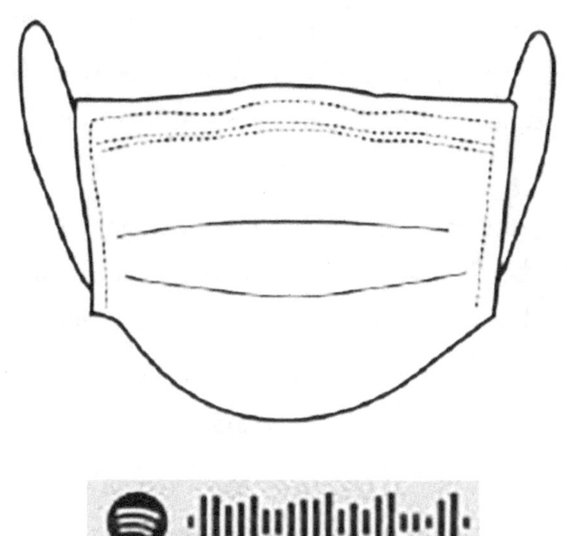

Chapter 19

OOPS OVER WHAT-IF'S

"And that's what happened, I am still very close to Neel, the strip website is literally very addicting and now this guy Rudh... I don't know what I am doing..." Paloma dragged deeply from the cigarette and completed the story.

She did not need any advice from her. She needs someone to talk to. About these things. Say it out loud. Shree took a few minutes to process. She did not reply immediately.

"Firstly you Need proper closure from Neel" Shree started. "You guys have been going on forever. Meet him or something and figure out what you both want" Paloma nodded

"Take a step back maybe after that, figure out who you are maybe. You seem very confused!" Shree spoke in a confused tone. She had a lot to digest in one go.

"Thanks for coming to my house, Satya is not letting me meet you outside," Paloma said.

"When will you realize he is not the guy? Maybe you need to see the love and then understand this is not the one"

Midnight. "Fix You" playing softly. Pretty drunk, still drinking. Blue light mixed with pink. She lit a cigarette. Doctor Dreamy wasn't online, so the online stripping site was of no use. So, what now? Started scrolling abruptly on social media.

"Meet me," she texted Neel.

"That's too risky Paloma and we know it all too well" Neel responded being reasonable.

He is right; Satya does not let her talk to Shree just because she is friends with Neel. And Shree is Paloma's oldest friend. He was in an active radiation zone for Satya, and if he knew they were still friends, let alone meeting, God knows what awaited her.

"I am ready to take the risk..." she pleaded. "Saturday, my place. Bring booze, and I will order food," Paloma texted.

And Neel couldn't say no. Neel couldn't ignore his heart anymore about her.

He recalls a few days ago when his dad had a heart attack, and he was at a loss about what to do. Thank God Paloma texted him that night. She stayed awake with him the entire night, offering support. "I've informed my dad; we'll be there whenever you need anything," she assured him. She was there in his weakest moments, a true friend after all these years.

They were the kind of friends who could meet after years and pick up right where they left off.

And that Saturday was no different...

"Check out my fancy cup," Paloma proudly displayed her very Pinteresty cup.

"No matter how fancy your cup is, those plastic ones will always be special," he remarked.

"Those days were lit," she reminisced.

"Indeed," he smiled.

"But honestly, I've never had a friend like you," she confessed.

"The feeling is mutual," he replied, pouring another drink on her balcony as the sun set, painting the sky in pretty colors.

"We have this understanding. It's rare... Like, I know you're an introvert," she began with a spark in her eyes.

"Am I?" he questioned.

"But somewhere, if something drastic happens to you, there's a part of you that wants to tell me about it," her enthusiasm contagious. "It always starts with 'bhai Janis Toh' (you know what happened)," he said with the same energy.

"We kinda grew up together," she said.

"In life, Neel needed a Paloma, and Paloma needed a Neel," he mused.

"The inside jokes that we have," she continued.

"It's as simple as that," he added.

"Do you remember that one time my mom came into our room without knocking?" she asked.

"Oh god! Your face, priceless," he chuckled.

"Because in my mind, I was somewhere else," she explained.

"In a parallel universe, I was making that face... but in a parallel universe, we probably are dating too," he joked.

"I believe if we met at a perfect time, we could have worked," she pondered.

"Maybe! You never know," he agreed.

"Were they worth it? Arjya? Nazia?" she questioned.

"They helped us grow," he acknowledged.

"But were they worth the effort we made?" she wondered.

"Not after how we were treated," he admitted.

"If we knew this, we might have dated each other once," she speculated.

"It would have been worth a shot," he agreed.

"It's sad. We didn't finish the story, Never mind" she said, recalling the story they started writing together.

"Some stories are best kept unfinished," he said, looking at the sky.

They sat together, looking at each other, and the evening grew darker. They felt a lot of things but didn't say much. The sky turned orange and purple as the sun set, making the moment more special. Memories and feelings filled the air, making their hearts feel heavy. It seemed like it was just them, caught in the beauty of the evening sky.

When he was leaving, she opened her main door, in a moment of vulnerability, he shut the door with a thud, and pulled her in a hug. The hug felt like a goodbye. Her breath fastened and his heart was beating aloud. She looked at him, both their hearts yearned for something more, but he was wearing a mask. The mask with a quote printed on it.

It says 'hope remains' What an irony

Later that night she sent him a text...

"Random thought:-

No, we didn't overcome what we had. We thought we did. We tried. It's not our fault maybe. This is how we were made. Maybe that's an excuse, maybe not. We are just like those particles that combine the moment they are left alone. Vulnerable. Perfect. But not willing to let our guard down. I know I can smell you. I knew in your head, you wanted to rip off my clothes and go ahead. It was not only my phone vibrating it was us repelling each other because that's the right thing to do. But the harder we were trying the closer we were. It was like gaining strength from that touch, from the warmth. I know what you thought while looking into my eyes in the darkness. That was all I was, carried away in the moment or maybe I was the moment? I cannot answer it all. It's like whenever we meet there's this electricity flowing around freely. The moment you touch that you know it's gonna vanish. It's like conserving the whole thing inside you and letting it flicker for a moment so that both of us know. Yeah, I know. I know that you know too. But that's too risky and we both are not that young. We want our roads to be parallel. But what to do about this longing? Do you want to break the rhythm because it sounds scary? Are we too perfect for each other? Or are we just two lost adults who happened to have sinister minds? Yeah, we still have it, and God knows how long it'll stay. The way you banged the door when I was about to open it and hugged me. Oh, I wished that no hope that remained but it was there like a wall between two heavily breathing nonteenagers, who longed for each other idk for how long. But hope remained between us like a wall so that we could walk. We walked our separate ways without turning back. But I swear it was not no strings attached. We knew we had each other's back. Your eyes were soft and so were mine. Goodbyes are sad but this was a thousand times amplifying.

Did you feel the same?

Or it was not kissing your best friend because it is lame?"

He replied eliminate "I felt this too, and no Paloma kissing my best friend is not lame... it's actually beautiful"

"Why does it feel like a sacrifice?" she questioned

"Maybe this is" he contemplated...

So the lines became parallel once again like railway tracks. They will interject someday, maybe not in the near future.

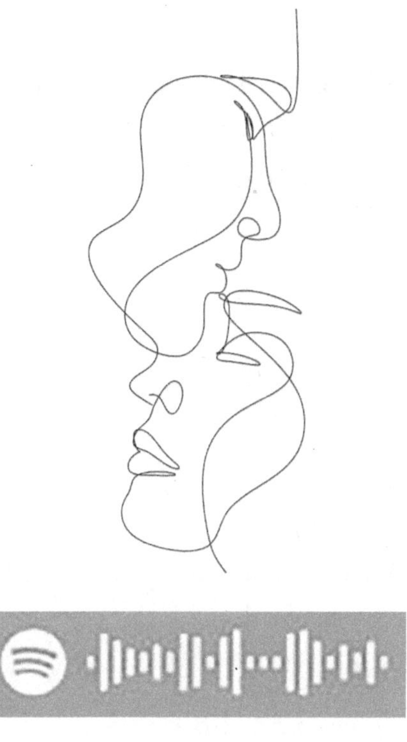

Chapter 20

THE FOREHEAD KISSES!

'Barish' by 'Anuv Jain'. A terrace with lush green plants. rhythmic Sound of rain falling. earthy smell of dry grass. And there he was...

A man, in a white shirt, snobby glasses, curly hair clueless...

Why?

Last night when she had a little too much to drink. than her usual two pegs, it's been months, she bid her goodbyes to Neel. The final goodbye. They are nothing but friends...

She needed to talk to someone, and the green dot beside one guy made her pulse quicken.

A rude recruiter... the man who gave her, her first job... later they connected over Facebook.

"Hi," she texted.

"Hey," came the reply.

"I hope I'm not disturbing... I was getting bored, saw you online, texted... kinda drunk," she confessed, hesitatingly overexplaining herself.

He subtly encouraged her, saying, "No, no. Tell me, what's up?"

"It's been a rough week... alcohol and drowning my sorrows," she painted herself as a sweet damsel in distress.

"It's part of our life, rough weeks... why sorrows though?" he inquired, prompting her to delve into the intricacies of her career and life choices.

"I closed a big deal, but at the last moment, it got canceled. My life sucks, my job sucks... how do you do it every day?" Paloma contemplated aloud.

It took him some time to digest the sudden outburst of emotions "Closures are not supposed to define your life..." he offered comfort.

"My life sucks totally... I am sorry if I am not behaving normally," she said will a conscious tone.

"It's alright, by the way... you are cute, so I won't mind," he flirted a little. he wanted to for a long time but that would have been unprofessional from his end.

"I wanna scream out loud, it's been a lot lately" she seized the window to pour out all her problems.

"You have to call me for that," but he is determined.

she got the memo now, and reciprocated, "I don't wanna scream at a person, especially a person who recruited me,"

"You can smile, and we can talk about it,"

"You actually scolded me for smiling at the interview, you remember?"

"Actually, I was getting distracted,"

"I was shitting myself; I was a backbencher, you know; I needed that job,"

"You were the only person I remembered amongst those thousands of people,"

"Well, am I that impactful?" she sought validation. "You are Paloma," he reassured.

"I wanna be good, you know, I wanna prove them wrong... the ones who underestimated me,"

"But you are already the best, who told you otherwise?"

"Am I a mess?"

"Quite the opposite."

"Be honest, please,"

"If this were mess, I would love this kind of mess."

She blushed a little.

"It's tough, being perfect... very tough... I tried," Paloma confessed, her voice heavy with vulnerability.

Unaware of the gravity, he tried cheering her up again, "You don't have to be perfect. Imperfections make you unique."

Paloma sighed, her fingers dancing across the keyboard. "You know I have a boyfriend, right?"

"Yes, I do," he typed back, his calmness evident even through the text.

"I am probably getting married in a year. I need to be perfect," she disclosed.

"Wow, congratulations," he wrote.

"Don't give me that, please, not now," guilt crept in. She poured herself another drink, took a sip, and saw the text:

"Don't drink more, talk to me."

Paloma was tired of pretending and sourja felt like a breath of fresh air. she could be unapologetically her in front of him, he did not judge he did not try to provide a solution, he just listened.

The night stretched on as they shared stories, laughter, and secrets. They spoke of dreams and fears, gradually peeling back the layers of their souls as the hours slipped away.

As dawn painted the sky with soft hues of pink and orange, exhaustion tugged at Paloma's eyelids. She yawned, her voice softened by drowsiness, "I should probably get some sleep."

he chuckled softly, his voice laced with tenderness, "Rest, Paloma. We can talk tomorrow."

Tomorrow The word hung in the air, filled with unspoken promises and unanswered questions. Paloma drifted off to sleep, thoughts of a mysterious stranger swirling in her mind.

Fluorescent lights illuminated his face as he stared at his reflection in the mirror. He let out a heavy sigh, can someone fall in love with a person in just 8 hours?

He lived in Pune, a distance of 1800 kilometers from her. Despite the geographical gap, the impulse was too strong. His fingers navigated through flight tickets, and he made her a promise to cook a cheese omelet for breakfast. Would she be able to meet him if he came to Kolkata? Was it the right decision? Was he falling for the wrong person again? With these thoughts swirling in his mind, he wanted to see the end of it. Pulling out his credit card, he booked a ticket from Pune to Kolkata.

The next day, as the rain poured like an orchestra outside, he found himself waiting nervously on Paloma's doorstep. He had flown from Pune to Kolkata just to meet her. Was it foolish? Perhaps.

"Why are you here?" Paloma asked with surprise.

Nerves and excitement coiled within him. Water droplets clung to his hair, his shirt drenched, as he climbed the stairs to her terrace following Paloma.

A storm of emotions brewed between them as he took a step closer, his heart pounding in his chest.

"I wanted to be here," he whispered. "To show you that sometimes imperfect choices can lead to extraordinary happiness."

He leaned in and her lips parted. It was one of her many fantasies, kissing on a terrasse. She closed her eyes and leaned in, but he kissed her on her forehead.

Did her heart melt a little? was she allowed to feel like that? It felt like a gush of wind in her windowless house...

She pushed him away from herself and went inside.

Sourjo stood there, confused. He never felt something like this before, for someone he just met.

Yes, his name was Sourjo...

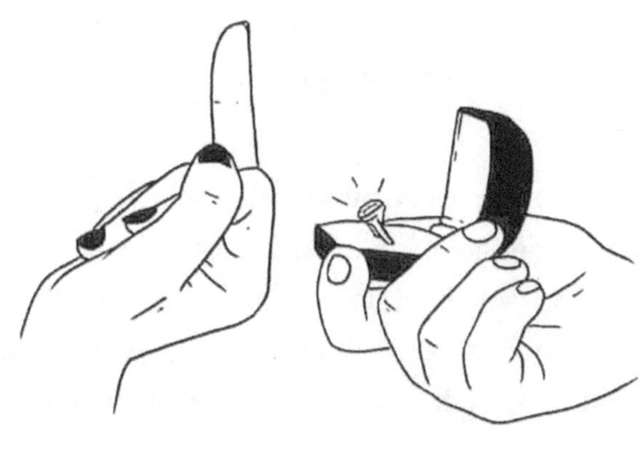

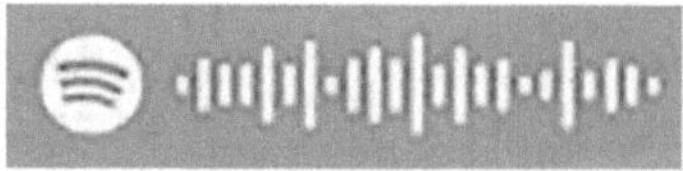

Chapter 21

CONGRATULATIONS...

"Paloma....come back," a voice, rich with resonance and charm, interrupted her. She turned around, realizing she had forgotten to end the video call. On the pixelated phone screen, a calm Sourjo continued to look at her, patiently waiting for her attention.

"Don't make this any harder than it already is" Paloma responded with an attempt to convince him but she was trying to convince herself.

Sourjo replied with a calm smile "You forgot your bindi."

And for a moment, she stood there perplexed for a while unable to process the gush of emotions she felt in a split second.

Have you ever met a person who can love you so much that they cannot hold you back, almost like when the wind flows and the dandelion doesn't hold back? A person who knows that you'll never be theirs, yet he helps you soar your wings and fly as high as you can. A person who smells like hope?

In all her years on Earth, Paloma had never encountered someone quite like him—simple yet wholesome. She longed for him to utter those words, "*Don't go,*" because deep down, she didn't want to. But was it too late to second guess her decision?

She was wearing a pink Kurti standing in front of a full length mirror. The room was aglow with warm golden light, casting a halo upon her silhouette.

On her 23rd birthday, Satya orchestrated a grand party where both families were to meet formally for the first time. Paloma, however, sensed the impending disaster, especially after the Neel and Rudh fiasco and the infamous strip website incident. Deep down, she knew she wasn't ready for this chaotic ride. Attempting to reason with Satya proved futile; it was as if he wanted to catch the train while it was already speeding away, securing a seat with a conveniently placed handkerchief. Paloma even went so far as to plead with Satya not to burden the celebration with expensive gifts,

Did he listen? Nope. He even dragged her shopping, wanting her to fit into the "ideal future daughter-in-law" mold. Paloma, being herself, opted for something sleeveless because, let's be real, Kolkata's April is hotter than a chili pepper.

She questioned his logic when Satya objected

"But your sister wears sleeveless dresses, what's wrong in this?"

Satya shut her down with a classic line, "All eyes will be on you, the future daughter-in-law, not her."

When her parents hurried, and she stepped into the car with a storm of emotions swirling inside her, she quietly rolled down the window, the wind caressing her face. Thoughts of the past swirled in her mind, fragments of memories she couldn't escape. Neel, Rudh, the strip website—they all resurfaced, reminding her of her hesitations about this engagement. And then, there was Sourjo... Who entered her life like a gush of cold wind...

The last two weeks felt like a dream. In the quiet moments they stole from the chaos of life, they found solace in each other's company. Whether it was sharing dreams over a cup of coffee or simply sitting in companionable silence, their bond deepened with every passing day. The secrecy of their meetings only added to the thrill, creating a world where it was just the two of them against the rest.

Oh, Sourjo's mom, the lady was like a warm blanket in a chilly room. From day one, he had this magical power of making Paloma feel like a long-lost friend. You know, the kind who accepts you with all your quirks and doesn't send you good morning texts as a reminder that you forgot to reply yesterday.

So, with Sourjo's family, it was all about real connections and unconditional acceptance. No pressure to fit into society's mold or become a 'perfect daughter-in-law who works but has time to do household chores'. It is natural to drift towards that warmth, leaving behind the conditional acceptance she felt from Satya's side.

Her chain of thoughts broke when the car stopped in front of a marigold-decorated gate. As they arrived, Paloma and her family were swept into a wave of greetings and celebrations. Handshakes, smiles, and laughter filled the air, masking her inner turmoil.

As Paloma stood beside Satya the engagement ceremony began with the priest chanting mantras, Satya extended his hand, adorned with an extravagant diamond ring. The room fell silent as all eyes turned toward Paloma. "Paloma, will you marry me?" Satya asked, his voice filled with anticipation.

Paloma hesitated for a moment, a thousand thoughts racing through her mind, unable to answer in words, she nodded.

Did her eyes soften? Well, everybody around her thought it was tears of joy...

She came home that day with a shiny ring on her finger, her parents wearing expressions caught between concern and obligation – all thanks to the hurried of events.

Amidst this emotional storm, a message silently sat in her archives: "Let me take you out for a birthday dinner?"

Chapter 22

CAN'T TALK BRB!

Paloma chose a sleek graphic crop top, that says: "They whispered in her ears, 'You can't sustain the storm.' She whispered back, 'I am the storm.' Paired with classic jeans, beachy waves cascading down her shoulders, and sneakers she was ready for the night.

"I'm going out with my cousins. They're excited about our engagement." The lies flowed effortlessly as she texted Satya.

"I am in front of Boulevard where are you" she texted standing at the entrance of the pub

"Look behind you," Sourjo said "Hi Storm... you look beautiful"

a playful grin on Paloma's face "Hi to you too"

They sat down and ordered some drinks, the kind of drinks that makes the conversation go smooth.

They choose a place which is very cozy, a small bar, away from the cacophony. Neon lights and 2000 Bollywood music. Nothing fancy. Paloma was quite frequent here. Good food and cheap alcohol.

"So, Miss Paloma, I know that you write. Your Instagram bio says you are an occasion wordsmith. I am willing to hear something if you don't mind" Sourjo said

"I mostly write in Bengali," she said being shy

"Try me" Sourjo winked

"Let me read a piece I wrote in English, that way, I get some criticism" Paloma gave a counter offer

He nodded.

Paloma looked at her notes, her face bright with the white lights of her phone, she started...

"It looked right through me

Deep into my soul

It broke me like ice.

It's coming back again

Haunting me through the night
My war had started.
There will come a time
When words will refuse to come
You'll feel Parts of your soul lost
And you will die searching for the missing Peaces.
The Oblivion of life.
The eternal nothingness.
You'll learn the value of a curve faked on a face
slowly emptied from the eyes long dead.
Why does it hurt?
What have I done?
I wasn't ready for this!!
Those demons
I feel them on every step I take
Getting stronger
Feeding on me
I can only watch
Chained to my thoughts
The room is getting darker

Nothing can come close to me anymore
No one can hear me scream!!!
What happened!!?
Am I lost?
All I hear is noises
People crying
Looking for a hand to hold
Losing their minds. breaking their heart
And all I could do is watch.
I see them
Walking with me
Hanging on to my shoulders
Whispering in my ears
I can't run away anymore
I'm giving up.
With the last few breath of sanity left in me
I'm writing my autobiography.
Nothing in this world lasts forever
Everything you hold close will be taken
So, if you wish live

Let no one in

Let nothing break you more than you already are.

Because in one moment of vulnerability

You will be in the depths of hell

Walking bare foot in flames of despite

Your soul will be stained forever.

I wish someone could hear me

Come for me

I know this will be tough

So, I won't ask you to try.

I'll be alright

I've tamed them before, and I will do it again

As long as it takes

I'm only sacred

I hope I won't be too late.

The worst part in this

You could hear the cracks

They learn to speak on their own

Reflecting the pain through the tears

Nothing holding them back

It’s like holding broken glass in your hand

More you try to hold them together

Deeper the wounds get.”

Sourjo kept looking at her throughout the reading. He couldn’t imagine what kind of pain each word carried. What could she have gone through to write something like this?

She looked at him “So... what do you think?” she asked

“I am speechless” was all he could say.

They ordered more drinks, and for the first time in a while, someone genuinely appreciated her art. Her art, in essence, served as her voice, expressing things she often struggled to put into words. As she gazed into his eyes, it felt like the cool breeze from the sea in the morning. Was she falling for him? Perhaps.

Regardless of love, that night, she felt an urge to escape. With each drink settling in her stomach, the calculated risk turned into a reckless mistake.

“What plans tonight?” Paloma asked with gloomy eyes

He in a flirty tone said “Why do I think the night is still young?”

“It can be” Paloma flirted back

A hint of concern on Sourjo’s face “But?”

“I don’t wanna go home...” Paloma pleaded

To be honest, Sourjo's heart couldn't refuse. He yearned for Paloma's presence, her smell, her touch

"Let me see if I can arrange a place to spend the night together," he said

"Crashing at my brother's place tonight. I'll call you tomorrow," she sent to Satya.

"I'm going to meet a friend of Satya's. Planning to stay over there," she explained to her mom.

He booked a suit in Marriot's for their night. In the dim glow of the city lights, Paloma and Sourjo stepped out of the pub and hailed a taxi. The air between them carried a certain energy, a quiet understanding that spoke volumes in the silence. As they settled into the backseat of the cab, the world outside seemed to blur into a backdrop. The driver adjusted the rearview mirror, to give them a little more privacy as their lips locked... such a gentleman.

Paloma almost believed she could outrun her problems, she just had to run very fast. What did she do her entire life? She tried fitting in, a concept her friends believed she was, a role the men in her life thought would be perfect, a box as Satya wanted. Right? Wrong? The lines had blurred long ego. What remained was an unsettling heart with a desire to be seen.

Satya did not allow her to shine brighter than he thought was required, Neel always outshined her with his own charms, Arjya got blinded by the bright lights and Rudh came just to warm his palms on a winter night with her warmth. Then how come, Paloma, was the villain of her own story? How come she was all wrong? Is the desire to be seen wrong?

Why does Sourjo make everything so easy? What was different in him that made Paloma not fear about her scars underneath? Why did he cast a glow on the darkest parts of her? Maybe to plant a seed... that will fill the cracks with sunflowers.

'Sleep on the floor' by 'the Lumineers'. Warm lights, a faint saint of lemon grass lingering.

Sourjo leaned in from the armchair. He delicately removed a strand of hair that teased Paloma's face, tucking it gently behind her ears. He looked into her eyes and said "You look so beautiful."

She leaned in yearning for a kiss, he touched her nose his is a playful manner, he brushed his perfectly made lips against hers. Cupping his face with both her hands, she surrendered.

It almost felt like a quenching thrust after being lost in a desert for days, maybe weeks. Her skin did not burn wish desires, yet her heart found quite a sense of fulfillment.

"Let's dance..." he said parting lips for a second.

She bit her lips and responded with a nod. Paloma couldn't ignore the flutter in her heart, a feeling that maybe, just maybe, this was the person she had been unknowingly searching for in everyone else.

And let me tell you, it was no salsa. If you could see them dancing, you might think they were on pills.

And when her feet hurt from all the dancing, he carried her to the bed. She rested her head on his neck, and he gently placed her on the bed. She opened her arms, inviting him into a warm hug. Resting his head on her chest, he gently traced lines with his fingers along the length of her arms. Paloma Playing with his hair. Maybe peace looks like this.

"Isn't it getting a little hot in here?" Paloma said with made up seriousness

Sourjo started to reply, "Should I reduce the AC tem..." but was cut off. Paloma, with a playful smile, took off her top.

Sourjo, responding with a smile, said, "I think it just got hotter." And removed his tee shirt.

Paloma never, NEVER sat naked in front of anyone with the lights on. The burden of what-ifs haunted her lifelong. But here, now, in this room, she found those thoughts powerless.

Sourjo slowly crawled up the bed, for a moment he couldn't focus on anything but her eyes. Slowly he caressed her face and gently kissed her cheeks. Their lips separated by a centimeter, and they could feel each other breath. Eyes closed with anticipation, she awaited the touch of his lips on hers. The moment didn't keep her waiting for long. He sealed both their souls with a deep kiss, reaching the depths of what lay underneath. His touch across her body sent shivers down her spine.

With a swift motion, he unhooked her bra, fondling her breasts with his other hand, with each touch, she felt like he was worshiping her, she felt like a goddess in his gaze... in no time she found her on top of him, moving swiftly, he untied her hair from the bun

"You look beautiful Paloma" his words made her smile, the kinda smile she hadn't had for years...

When their breaths stopped racing, their mind stopped thinking, they lay naked under the roof. They did not find the aggressive urge to hug each other or turn their backs to each other. They simply lay naked holding hands...

Paloma awoke to the persistent buzzing of her phone, and the sight of 'Satya' on the screen served as a stark reminder. "Hello," she answered, attempting to sound composed.

"Where are you, Paloma?" came his urgent question.

"Why?" she responded, a hint of panic underlying her voice.

"Your mom called," he informed her plainly.

"Can't talk. BRB," she hurriedly hung up,

The End

www.ingramcontent.com/pod-product-compliance
Lightning Source LLC
LaVergne TN
LVHW041210150826
845673LV00001B/344

* 9 7 9 8 8 9 2 3 3 3 9 1 7 *